Naughty Housewives

A Novel

Ernest Morris

Good 2 Go Publishing

Naughty Housewives
Written by Ernest Morris
Cover design: Davida Baldwin
Typesetter: Mychea
ISBN: 978-1-943686-53-7

Copyright ©2016 Good2Go Publishing
Published 2016 by Good2Go Publishing
7311 W. Glass Lane • Laveen, AZ 85339
www.good2gopublishing.com
https://twitter.com/good2gobooks
G2G@good2gopublishing.com
www.facebook.com/good2gopublishing
www.instagram.com/good2gopublishing

Once again I have turned a vision in my head into a reality on paper. It started with *Flipping Numbers*, and it won't stop until I have reached out to the minds and hearts of everyone across the world. *Naughty Housewives* was one of my toughest challenges because it made me have to think outside the box and create characters that would make you visualize yourself as being.

I thank God first and foremost, for blessing me with this gift of being able to write novel after novel and continuing to do it successfully. No one knows the struggle that writers go through to constantly put out storylines that will keep readers intrigued and wanting more. It truly takes time and dedication, and I, along with the other authors, appreciate your support.

Thank you so much!!

Acknowledgments

First and foremost, God (Allah), please continue to direct me on the right path so I can not only become a vessel that you work through, but also someone that others can become inspired by. Amen!!

Life's journey has taken me to places that made me sit back and question what I am really here for and why this is happening to me. I had to really evaluate myself and realize that all the negative things that have happened to me had a sole purpose: that was to change me from a lil boy to a man. Just 'cause I'm an adult doesn't mean I was living like one.

Here's something people never knew about me: When I lost my mother (Jacqueline Morris) when I was fourteen, and then my sister (Conyia Morris) a year later, I went into a state of depression. I even contemplated suicide. People always saw E.J. smiling on the outside, but inside, I was a complete wreck emotionally, as well as spiritually. I thought how could there be a God if he took two of the most important people in my life away from me. There are times when I am alone and I think about my mom and sister, and I tear up because I miss them so much. Even till this day I still do. I now realize, though, everyone is born with an expiration date. God (Allah) has a bigger plan for every one of us. I love you Mommy and Connie; REST IN PEACE!

Anyway, what I'm trying to say is, it took me all these years to see and reach my full potential in life. A man without a vision for his future will always return to his past. I'm not going backward, I'm moving forward. I can't no longer be that person I used to be. You will get to know the real me in my autobiography, *One Man's Triumph*, coming soon.

I was blessed with four beautiful children: Le'Shea Burrell, Sahmeer Morris, Demina Johnson, and Shayana Morris, and I never really had the chance to be in their lives because of my actions in the past. Any man can make a baby, but it takes a real man to step up and be a father. I wasn't that man. I want them to know that I'm gonna spend the rest of my time left on this earth, with some help from them, to be a good, if not great, father. There is a light at the end of the tunnel, and I'm heading toward it.

I dedicate this book to not only my children, but also their mothers: **Brandi Burrell, Kendra Funchez, Meena Johnson,** and **Nakisha Cousin,** for being the strongest women I ever have known, and for their unconditional motherly love. Ya'll sacrificed everything to raise the best children in the world. If it was up to me, every day would be Mother's Day.

I also dedicate this book to my brothers: **Kevin (Chubb) Morris** and **Sedric (Walid) Morris.** We never had the brotherly bond we were supposed to have, because we were always apart, but time heals all wounds.

To all my extended family: Loveana, Cynthia, Theresa, Kita, Trina, Gianni, Dwunna, Leneek, Kimmy, Alona, Lyric, Jamie, Zyrinah, Dom, Pam, Nyia, Myra, Symira,

Jigga, Neatra, Dee Dee, Sharon, Aleesha, Damein, Nafeese, Shy, Phylis, Shot Gun, Eric, Sherman, Eddie, Maurice, Rasheed, Frank, Ty, Donte, Chris, Ed, Vettie, Torey, Zy, Arnold, Christian, Baheem, Gavin, Nay Nay, Renea, Tia, Sherry, Shawn, Seiara, Layah, Ci Ci, etc. Thank you for your support in making me a better man.

To all my aunts and cousins: Peggy, Katherine, Cathy, Mildred, Sister, Tee, Cindy, Bobby, Steve, June, Gilbert, ade, Ottis, Lil Man, Fat Man, Meka, Antoinette, Sinky, Vanessa, Glenda, Sareeta, Mike Mike, Stephenie, Brandy, Pooh, Link, Cinquetta, The Twins, Jacon, Tasha, Bo, Dee, Tysheka, Barry, Pooch, Angie, Meek, Eric, James, Ronald, Keith, Tony, Michael, Darnell, Toga, Chrissy, Brenda, Tranea, Felicia, Nygel, Auntie, Peanut, Janell, Loretta, Ray, Etta, Nikki, Mike, Danielle, Kenyetta, Stanetta, Rasheeda, G.I., Margaret, Rubar, etc. There are so many of you that I know I am forgetting, and I apologize for it. I really want to thank all of you for just being the people you are. My eyes are open, and now I truly see what everyone means to me.

To my best friends: Yahnise, Harmon, you already know that words cannot explain your loyalty to me, and mine to you. Keep doing your thing, ma, and let the haters keep hating.

To everyone at the Cheesecake Factory: A.J. Katz, John, Shelly, Arnold, Kayla, Marcus, Jade, Will, Evani, Lope, Dom, Rhonda, Christina, Pamela, Janette, Morgan, Tia, Jalisa, Ty, Bill, London, Melissa, Toya, Stacks, Dawn, Sarah, Torey, Jackie, Stacy, Ryan, Leanne, Edward, Nestor, Nancy (both), Mia, and everyone else that I missed—you know who you are—thanks for letting me be a part of the winning team.

I want to give a shout out to all my Passyunk family. They took the buildings but left the name, memories, and love.

To Omar, Piper (Pike), and Knowledge (South Philly), that door is about to open up to those prison walls. It just takes patience and hope. Each one of you inspired me in different ways. I want you to know that I will never forget you. Stay strong in there, and I will see you on the other side when we hit those Passyunk reunions up.

Special thanks to Worlds and Josh for staying on me to complete this. I hope that this will be another great one.

Naughty Housewives

Sasha never had a chance to say anything to her husband the next morning, because he was already gone. She hated going to bed by herself and then waking up the next day still alone. It had been going on for the past two months, and it was starting to make her wonder what was really going on with her husband. Sasha just wanted someone to hold her at night or in the morning when she woke up.

Fed up with the whole thing, Sasha decided that she would get even some day. She called the diner to place an order because she was hungry. While she waited for her food, her pussy began to tingle. It had been over a month since she and her husband had been intimate. She sat down on the bed and lifted her gown, exposing her clean-shaven vagina. She started rubbing her clit with one hand while pinching her hardened nipples with her other. Her pussy became so wet that each time she stuck two fingers inside and pulled them out, her sweet juices would follow, hitting the sheets. It didn't take long for her to come to her first orgasm, but she needed more.

She reached into her nightstand and pulled out her vibrator, hoping that it would help satisfy her urges. As she stuck it inside, it immediately sent chills throughout her body. Sasha was enjoying her masturbation session, until the doorbell rang. She tried to continue concentrating on what she was doing, but the sound of the bell made it hard.

"Ugh, not now," she screamed, getting off the bed. She grabbed her robe and proceeded downstairs to see who had interrupted her from reaching her second climax.

When she opened the door, her pussy became even wetter at the sight of the stud standing before her. He stood five foot nine, with a nice build, which told her that he worked out occasionally. He looked like he was mixed with black and Hispanic, and Sasha even noticed the bulge in his pants.

"How much do I owe you?" she stated, snapping out of the trance she was in. She looked away so that he couldn't see the lust in her eyes.

3

"That will be $22.75, miss," the deliveryman said.

She told him to hold on as she rushed back up to her bedroom to retrieve her wallet. When she came down, the young man was still standing by the door. The sight of his erection made her want to invite him up to her room for some pleasure, but she didn't know when her husband would be returning.

"Keep the change," she said, passing him a fifty-dollar bill. His eyes got wide at the thought of the tip she was giving him. "Do you work there all the time?"

"Yes, I'm the only driver that works this side of town. We have another driver, but he works the other side. If you ever order again, most likely it will be me bringing your food. Have a nice day, ma'am," he said, heading out the door.

"Good to know, and you do the same," Sasha said, shutting the door. She was so hot now that she wasn't even hungry anymore. She sat the food on the kitchen table, then went back to her room, this time with a new mission in mind.

She closed her eyes, slid two fingers between her thighs, and thought of the delivery guy. She thought of him kissing her on the forehead, then working his way down to her breasts. He gripped both of them and squeezed them together as he took turns sucking on each nipple.

He gently bit her top lip, sucking on it. Tugged at her nipples, rolling each one between his thumb and forefinger. She felt his cock get even harder.

Sasha wet her finger and ran it up the lips of her pussy and imaged it was his tongue, wetting the wings of her labia, feeling them flutter and spread. Her fingers were circling her clit and flicking it. Blood rushed to her head, and to her clit, making her feel dizzy.

Sasha felt the head of his cock bouncing against her thigh as he climbed on top of her, positioning himself, ready to enter. She turned on her side to accommodate him, bending the top leg at the knee, like a dancer doing the cancan, to give him a clear path to her ever-so-moist pussy.

The deliveryman took his cock in his hand and guided it into her pussy. He pushed into it, just enough to wet the tip. He then pulled out and slid the head up the pussy, making her slick with her own juices.

He slid back into her just enough to bury the tip, and held it there, teasing her a little. Sasha was so horny at the dream that she started moaning from pushing two, then three fingers deep into herself.

As she continued to think about the stud, she imagined his cock stretching her hole, and she felt her pussy close around the head. He began to pound away, and she could feel it pressing against her pelvis.

Sasha was up to the joint now, and moving toward the knuckle, sinking her fingers as deep as they would go. Her fingers were slick with her own juices, thick and sticky, and white as snow.

As she thought of him pounding away, she suddenly felt herself about to cum. She felt the urge building up inside of her and couldn't stop it. She didn't want it to either. She wanted to explode so bad, that she started going faster and faster. As she busted all over her hand, she could hear her husband call out to her. She snapped out of her daydream but stayed in the bed naked, hoping he would come and give her what she needed, the real thing.

Marcus walked into the bedroom and acted like he didn't even notice that she was lying there. He had come back to pick up the paperwork he left on the nightstand.

"You don't have to cook tonight because I'll be at the gym late. I will pick up something while I'm there," he stated.

Sasha was pissed because she had planned a romantic dinner for them. Now she would once again be eating alone tonight. After he left, she decided to call her next door neighbor and best friend, Michelle, to see what she was doing.

A few rings later, someone answered the phone. Sasha could hear a lot of arguing in the background and assumed Michelle was arguing with her husband about something.

"Hi, Mrs. Sasha, you want to speak to my mother?" Mike asked.

Mike was Michelle's eighteen-year-old son. He was home for summer vacation from college. He and Sasha's son were best friends, just like she was with his mom.

"Yes, but I can call back if she is busy."

"It's the same ol' stuff. My dad has to work late today, so he won't be home for dinner, and she is pissed. When is Sahmeer coming home?" he asked.

"He said he's gonna stay down there until next week so he can bring his girlfriend back with him so we can meet her," Sasha replied.

"Oh, okay, well I'll let her know that you called, and tell Mr. Marcus that I said hello."

"I will. Just tell her to call me whenever she is free," Sasha said before ending the call.

She sat the phone back on the charger and headed for the bathroom to take a shower. Since she would be all alone today, she decided to go out to the mall and enjoy herself.

She hoped that Michelle called before she left so she could

join her.

WO

Carla realized that she was going to be late for practice, so she called her instructor to let him know.

"Hey, Rapheal, I'm running a little bit behind, but I'll be there soon," Carla said, putting her headset on so she wouldn't get a ticket for driving while on the phone.

"You know that's not a problem. You're the only one scheduled for today anyway. I will see you when you get here," Rapheal replied.

"Okay, see you in a few," Carla told him before ending the call.

Rapheal was Carla's piano instructor. He was a very good player, so when she saw him teaching at the community center, she requested his services. He had been giving her private lessons for just over a month now. The lessons were two hours long, twice a week. She wanted more time, but she had to respect the fact that she wasn't the only one; he had other students as well.

Twenty minutes later Carla was at the center and ready to start her lessons. When she stepped out of the car, she noticed that her and Rapheal's cars were the only cars in the lot. That usually didn't mean anything, because a lot of people would walk there to play basketball and work out. For some reason, though, today felt a bit different. When she walked inside, the place looked deserted. Nobody was playing ball or working out in the gym. She walked straight to the back of the center, where Rapheal was waiting.

"Hey, glad you finally made it. Now we can get started on the new song I was telling you about," he said, not even turning around to see who came in, because he already knew.

Carla took off her jacket and sat down next to him on the stool. He began playing the new song so she could see the chords he was playing. After going through it once, he stopped and looked at her for the first time.

"Your husband will love you after he hears this song. I just hope you don't have any plans on getting out of bed, because that's where the two of you will be for the whole weekend," Rapheal stated.

That statement made Carla blush. She had been trying to do something special for her husband for quite some time now. When she started these lessons, she knew right then that this would be a surprise.

"I'll be ready for whatever may come my way," she replied with much confidence.

"So let's see what you've learned so far," he said, giving her the signal to start playing the piece she just heard.

Carla began playing the song with such efficiency that you would have thought she had been playing for years. The melody of the song had her lost in her own world. Rapheal stared at her the whole time. He secretly had a crush on her, but who wouldn't. She was truly beautiful.

She was five six, 135 pounds, which made her a little petite. She had long reddish hair that came to her lower back and gave proof that she was mixed with something. She was Italian and Creole and could speak three different languages. Carla had perky 36D breasts, and those features are what had him hypnotized by her beauty. He knew she was forbidden fruit, and all he could do was look and not touch. There were many nights that he would be at home in bed and have wet dreams of what it would be like to be inside her moist walls. He imagined himself licking every part of her perfectly structured body, from head to toe.

"So did I do okay?" Carla asked, snapping him back to reality. "Did I end it the right way, like I was supposed to?"

Rapheal never even heard the ending, so he didn't know if it was right or wrong. He was trying to figure out why this beautiful woman had him this way.

"You did great," he said trying not to let her know the truth. "This is our last session, and you, my dear, are truly ready to perform for your man."

She reached into her purse and pulled out her credit card. "You can charge the payment to this card."

"This one was on the house. You don't owe me anything for this session. Just go home and make your husband a very happy man."

"Thank you so much. I may even require your services some more in the future if everything works out like it is supposed to. Our anniversary is coming up soon, and I would like to learn how to play his favorite song. It will be a real surprise to him."

"Well, in that case, I wish you all the best. I hope that I will have a chance to see you again so that we can practice some more," he said.

16

He walked over to Carla and gave her a more than friendly hug. She could feel his manhood rubbing against her pelvis. She felt her panties become moist. As much as she wanted to break free from his embrace, her body wouldn't allow her to.

Rapheal placed his hand on the small of her back, and he brushed the other hand over her ass, pulling her even closer to him. She looked up to say something but was met with his lips touching hers. Carla gave in, opening her mouth, inviting him to put his tongue inside. They began to french kiss passionately, and he started squeezing her ass cheeks together.

Suddenly Carla realized that what she was doing was wrong and pulled away from him slightly. Rapheal also knew that he had just crossed the line, and let go of her.

"I'm sorry, Carla. I got caught up in the moment, and I will never let that happen again," he said, holding his head down.

"We both made a mistake, but we corrected it before it went too far. Let's just forget about it like it never happened," she replied, grabbing her jacket and heading for the door. He watched as the most beautiful woman he had ever seen walked out of the studio.

When she closed the door, she leaned back up against it and sighed. As much as she wanted to feel him inside her, she couldn't cross that line, or bring herself to do so. She hopped in her car and headed home. Her phone rang while she was waiting at the light.

"Hello," she said, seeing that it was her husband's office calling.

"Hey, Carla, how is everything going?" Symira asked.

18

"I'm good, just stopping by the market to grab something for dinner tonight. Is everything okay?" she asked, turning into the shopping center.

"Yes, your husband just wanted me to let you know that he will be running late. He's in a conference meeting with the president and governor. They scheduled it at the last minute, so there was nothing he could do."

"Thank you, Symira, for calling. I guess I don't have to rush now. Tell him I'll see him when he gets home," Carla said, happy that she had more time to prepare for tonight.

"Okay, I'll talk to you later," Symira replied, ending the call.

Carla grabbed the items that she would need for dinner, then headed home. Tonight was going to be a special night, and she was also going to let her husband know that they had a new life coming into the world. She was six weeks pregnant.

* * *

"So did you inform my wife that I would be coming home late tonight?" Morgan asked, coming out of his office.

Symira looked up from the computer screen momentarily and said, "Yes sir. She was at the market," but she didn't say anything else.

Morgan was assistant for the governor of Pennsylvania and was very well known in the political world. He had a master's in public relations and an MBA in sociology. Graduating at the top of his class, he worked for the mayor of Philadelphia, then went on to become the governor's most trusted assistant. Since it was the governor's first term in office, after beating out Corbin, who only served one term, he wanted to make sure that he stayed for the long haul. Morgan was a strategic genius when it came to politics. That was the reason the mayor let him go. He figured Morgan would be more valuable to him there. So far, it was all working out for both parties.

"Good, so are you ready to go?" he asked, putting his suit jacket on. "Our reservations are for seven o'clock. That gives us about forty-five minutes to get there."

"Let me save these schedules for next week, and grab my purse," she replied.

Morgan watched as she finished up on what she was doing, then stood up from the desk. She bent down to grab her purse, when she felt someone grab her waist from behind.

"Mmmmmm, is that your car keys, or are you happy to see me?" she whispered, leaning into his grasp.

"Take your pick, but if you guess wrong, you lose."

"Then I guess I will have to say that you're happy to see me," she responded, grinding against his crotch.

Morgan spun her around and lifted her up onto her desk. They started kissing as Symira began to unbuckle his pants. She pulled his penis out and started massaging it, bringing it to full erection.

"We don't have time for foreplay, so lean back," he said, pulling her panties to the side.

Symira kicked off her shoes and leaned back on the desk, spreading her legs as wide as they could go. Morgan looked at her neatly trimmed pussy then licked his lips. He entered her hot, wet walls with ease.

"Oh my goodness," Symira moaned, pulling his body into hers as he began to slowly pump in and out. "You feel so good, baby. Don't stop."

Symira was light skinned and was very beautiful. She stood five five and was 125 pounds, and had jet black hair that came just past her shoulders, nice C-cup breasts, and a smile that could make any man blush. That is why Morgan hired her, besides the fact that he was having an affair with her.

He met her when she was working at Starbucks in Center City. Morgan would stop there every morning and order the same thing. After two days, she had his order down to a science. When he walked in, she had his coffee and cream cheese bagel already waiting for him. He asked her if she wanted to work for him one day, because his other secretary left on maternity leave. Symira accepted the job the next day and had been there ever since.

"I can't wait until we're in Washington next weekend. Then I can have you all to myself for two whole days," he whispered, pumping faster and harder, trying to hurry up and release his semen.

"When are you going to leave your wife?"

"We've talked about this before, ma, as soon as you leave your husband," he answered while bringing himself to an orgasm.

"I can't just ask for a divorce without reason," she replied as she fixed her clothes.

"And neither can I, so we both have to wait patiently until the time is right," Morgan stated. "Now let's go enjoy the rest of the night. I don't want to stay out too late and make her suspicious."

* * *

The next morning Carla woke up to an empty bed. She glanced over to see if her husband had even slept in it last night. To her surprise, his side of the bed hadn't even been touched. She got up and went into the bathroom to brush her teeth and wash her face.

When she came out of the bathroom, the smell of turkey bacon and cheese eggs filled her nostrils. Carla slipped her robe on, then followed the smell to the kitchen.

"Good morning, sleepy head, are you hungry?" Morgan asked, setting the plate of food on the table. "I was gonna bring you breakfast in bed, but since you're up, we might as well eat down here. Have a seat, beautiful."

Carla sat down at the table, but she was still wondering where he was last night and why wasn't he in bed. She thought that this was his way of apologizing for something he had done. He had on his slippers and a pair of shorts, which led her to believe that he was at least in their room this morning.

"I got home a little after one this morning, and I slept on the couch after finishing the speech for the governor," he lied.

Morgan actually didn't get in until after four. He was out all night with Symira, who also had to lie to her husband. They ended up going to a hotel when they left the restaurant for a nightcap of wild sex. He didn't know it, but while he thought he had gotten away with the lie, someone had seen him at the hotel with his mistress.

"This smells good," Carla said, biting a piece of toast. She then ate a fork full of the cheese eggs and home fries.

"I'm free today. Would you like to go see a movie and maybe afterward we could go out to Penn's Landing and have dinner on the Spirit of Philadelphia?"

Carla's anger that she felt when she first woke up this morning was suddenly replaced with excitement. She could tell him the good news and play the song that she learned when they returned.

"What time should I be ready?" she said.

"We can catch the 7:45 movie and then go over and have dinner, unless you want to eat first?" he replied rubbing her shoulders.

"That sounds good, but let's eat first because I still have a surprise for you later," she responded.

Morgan gave her a kiss on the forehead and then went upstairs to take a shower. He breathed a sigh of relief knowing that he had just escaped a controversial argument. He shut the bedroom door so that he could call Symira and let her know that he would be spending the day with his wife. He knew she would probably be doing the same because they fucked up last night by staying out too late. As soon as he hung up with her, he headed for the shower.

Carla heard the shower running when she came upstairs, and decided to join him. She let her robe hit the ground, then took off her nightgown, stepping into the shower. She grabbed the sponge and started washing Morgan's back.

Morgan closed his eyes and relaxed his muscles as he felt her hands all over his body. It started with his back and ended up with his manhood being stroked. He quickly

28

turned around and began passionately kissing Carla. She continued to stroke his penis with one hand while massaging her clit with the other.

"I missed you so much last night," Carla mumbled, taking a breath.

"Show me how much then," he replied.

Carla got down on her knees and took him into her mouth. The warm sensation drove him crazy. She started off by blowing on the tip, then licking up and down the shaft of his dick.

"Mmmmmm, that's right, baby. Show him how much you miss him," he said, grabbing the back of her head. He began fucking her mouth like it was her pussy.

When he felt his balls stiffening up, he lifted Carla up and turned her around. She placed her hands on top of the shower door as he entered her from behind. She arched her

29

back, sticking her ass in the air to give him a clear view of her hairless vagina.

Morgan started off slow stroking, then sped up while pinching her nipples and sucking on the back of her neck. Next, he spread her ass cheeks apart and stuck his thumb in her hole. That sent shock waves through her body, and she started convulsing as her cream spilled out all over his dick. A few pumps later, he ejaculated inside her walls, and the two washed up again before getting out.

Feeling relieved, Carla cleaned the house from top to bottom with no help from him. She couldn't wait until tonight so she could break the good news to him.

Three

Sasha and Michelle had just left the AT&T store, because Michelle needed a new phone. She had broken hers arguing with Kevin. They decided to grab some lunch, since neither of them ate breakfast this morning. They were sitting at a table waiting for someone to take their order, when Sasha decided to ask about yesterday's argument.

"So why were you and Kevin arguing this time?"

"You don't understand. He's gone for weeks, and I'm left home all alone. He can't be working that much," Michelle said, feeling the anger starting to come back again. "Don't you ever wonder what your husband is out there doing when he takes those trips?"

Sasha knew exactly what her friend was talking about. She felt the same way. Both their husbands were NBA players. They both had been in the league for fifteen years now and were getting close to their careers being over.

"I do think about it all the time, but I also have to trust him to do the right thing," she replied.

She didn't want to tell her friend how she fantasized about the delivery boy earlier today. That would only make her suspicions even greater and would prove her to be right. So for now, she was going to keep that dream to herself.

"They're always at the office going over film or in the gym practicing for the next game. We only go to the home games or the ones that are in the area. Why can't we travel to the West Coast with them?" Michelle questioned.

"Because we have to take care of home, Michelle. We knew what we were getting into when we first started dating them in college. There's going to be days that don't go as we want, but it's just a part of marriage," Sasha said.

"You make it seem so simple. That vibrator must keep that kitty tamed while Marcus is gone."

That made both women bust out laughing, taking some of the tension away. They needed that laugh before their minds started playing tricks on them.

"It does its job, but there's nothing like the real thing. It can only do so much," Sasha said, smiling. "I need to be wrapped in that strong muscular body, getting my hair sweated out."

That comment sent chills throughout Michelle's body. It had been two weeks since she felt that kind of passion. She was tired of using dildoes and clit massagers. She needed some body heat as well.

"They are going to Washington tonight for tomorrow's game. How about we surprise them at the hotel?" Michelle said.

"Look at your hot ass. That's why we had our sons at the age of eighteen in the first place. Remember that night?" Sasha said as she reminisced back to the night her and Michelle hooked them in.

March 1997

"It's morning, and we slept the night away. It happened, now we can't turn back the hands of time," Shirley Murdock sang on the radio as two couples laid in two beds at the Hilton Hotel. They had been sneaking off every weekend for the last month since going to see the two boys play basketball. Marcus and Kevin were juniors at the University of North Carolina while Michelle and Sasha were freshmen.

They all met at a frat party and realized that they were from the same city. The only difference was Sasha and Michelle were from North Philly, and Marcus and Kevin were from West Philly.

Every time they would have sex, Sasha would secretly watch the way Kevin's dick would move in and out of her best friend. Marcus was packing in that department too, but he seemed to only last for ten minutes before it was over.

35

Sometimes she wouldn't even reach her orgasm, so he would eat her pussy until she got hers. She preferred that anyway. His tongue was like a snake on her clit. He definitely knew how to please a woman orally.

As she lay there next to Marcus, who was asleep now, she kept her eyes on the action in the next bed. The two of their bodies moved in sync as if they were one. Michelle's ass was in the air while Kevin was deep stroking her from behind. Sasha's hand mysteriously ended up inside her panties, rubbing her clit. She closed her eyes, listening to her friend moaning.

She moved her fingers faster and faster until she felt herself reaching her orgasm. When she came, she let out a soft moan. She opened her eyes, hoping that no one had heard her. When she looked over toward them, Michelle was now riding him. Kevin was looking over at her smiling. Sasha felt embarrassed as she turned over, wrapping up in the sheets. Minutes later, she heard both of them cumming in unison. Sasha fell asleep with those thoughts on her mind.

The next day, Sasha woke up first, then reached over to wake her friend up. She shook her a couple of times before she finally opened her eyes.

"Hmmm, what time is it?" Michelle said, stretching.

"Shhh, don't wake them up," Sasha whispered. "Did you do it last night?"

"Yeah, did you?"

"Yep! Now let's just hope that it works. They are our meal tickets from going back to nothing," Sasha replied.

"I feel kind of bad, though. I don't think they would go to the NBA and forget about us. Kevin is already saying that he loves me."

37

ERNEST MORRIS

Sasha just shook her head at her naive friend. She really thought that he told her that because he meant it. You would be surprised the words that come out of people's mouths in the heat of passion.

"They will say anything to get what they want. Now that they got it, they can up and leave at any time. We've just insured ourselves that no matter what, we still get a piece of the pie."

They both had poked holes into the condoms they used last night so that they could get pregnant. Sasha was the one who had come up with the idea, and even though she had regrets, Michelle still was part of the plan.

"What are you two whispering about?" Marcus asked, waking up. He turned over and started rubbing Sasha's back.

38

"Oh nothing, we have to go take care of some things today," she replied, getting up and going to the bathroom to take a shower.

"We do too! We have to take our physicals for the upcoming draft next weekend," Marcus said, throwing a pillow at Kevin to wake him up. "Let's go, cuz. We have to be there in a couple of hours, and you know we can't be late."

Kevin hopped up and grabbed his clothes before heading into the other room to take a shower. Marcus was getting his stuff together when Michelle got out of bed in her bra and panties. Just like Sasha, Michelle had a flawless body. The only difference between them was she was a little thicker than Sasha.

She walked toward the bathroom like Marcus wasn't even sitting there. He just stared at her body, mesmerized by how perfect her ass was. He wondered what it would feel like bouncing up and down his shaft. Just the thought had his dick brick hard. Sasha had locked the door so Michelle couldn't get in. She turned around to go sit back on the bed to wait, when she noticed his erection.

"Damn, you need to fix yourself," she said, pointing at his dick trying to poke a hole in the sheet.

Marcus smiled, and suddenly stood up, exposing himself to her. He could tell that she didn't expect that, and he started blessing her with a sensual striptease. He walked over toward Michelle. She looked at him like he was crazy.

"Marcus, stop playing before Sasha or Kevin come back," she replied, trying to move away from him.

He grabbed a fistful of her hair and looked into her face. When he pressed his exposed penis on her pelvis, she initially began to get moist in her panties.

40

"They are going to be at least five to ten minutes. That's enough time to show you what you could have had."

Michelle was speechless as she struggled like hell to break free from his grasp, but her legs said something different because they didn't move.

"You are crazy," she whispered.

Instead of responding, Marcus let her hair go, got on his knees, and sucked the sticky folds of her pussy lips through her panties. He pulled them to the side, and the creamy juice from her G-spot ran down her thighs as he began to aggressively lick her clit. Instantly, Michelle started shaking.

"Ummm, wait, we can't do this," she moaned, grabbing his head.

He turned her around and kissed her ass while his tongue found her hole. Michelle didn't know what to do as the pleasure won over her better judgment. Marcus didn't know what to do as the pleasure won over her better judgment. Marcus bent her over the front of the bed, still holding her panties to the side. She looked over her shoulder to get a good look at his beautiful dick. It looked to be more than ten inches. In fact, it was so big that it didn't look real. She felt him rubbing the head between her legs. When he pushed it inside of her wet walls, she closed her eyes and gasped for air.

"This is what you missed out on," he said, slowly going in and out. "I knew your pussy was good from the way Kevin was tearing it up."

Instead of saying something, Michelle took her arm, reached above her head, and grabbed the back of Marcus's neck, causing him to ram his entire dick into her, forcing her walls to collapse. She gripped the sheets on the bed as he pounded away. Marcus thrust his pelvis and worked his groin muscles with everything he had. Michelle tried to throw her ass back at him to make him cum faster, but she felt her own orgasm coming.

Just as they both reached their climax, the shower water turned off, causing them to stop and fix themselves. Michelle grabbed the sweatpants she wore last night and threw them on. Marcus put on his boxers and got back under the sheet. Just as Michelle had pulled her shirt down, Sasha walked out of the bathroom.

"Girl, you not going to take a shower first?" she said, drying her hair with the towel, looking at her friend already dressed. She gave Michelle a wink.

"Your ass had the door locked and was taking too long. I thought you fell in the drain." Michelle smirked. She picked up her overnight bag and headed toward the bathroom. She turned back to see Marcus staring at her. She rolled her eyes and closed the door.

"You better get up and get ready before Kevin comes back," she said, putting on her clothes. He got up and rushed to get dressed.

Four weeks later, Sasha was in her bathroom taking a pregnancy test to see what the outcome would be. After five minutes, she picked up the stick, and a smile crept across her face. It read two lines, which meant positive. She quickly dialed Michelle's number to see what happened with her test. Michelle's also came back positive.

When they told the boys the news, neither one of them could believe they got caught up like that. It took some time, but they ended up accepting the fact that they had kids on the way. Two months after they both got drafted into the Sixers, they proposed and married the girls.

44

"Yeah, I wish we would have went about it a different way, but one thing for sure, I don't regret my baby," Michelle said.

Sasha snapped back to the present and replied, "Neither do I. I thank God every day for blessing me with such a beautiful son."

"Look who just walked in," Michelle said, looking at the entrance to the food court.

Sasha looked toward the entrance, to see Carla come strolling in with a couple of bags in her hands. They all lived in the same gated community in Lower Merian. Because of her husband's status, people had the assumption that she thought that she was better than everybody else. She spotted them sitting at the table and walked toward them.

"Please don't try and make a scene right now. Try to be nice unless she says something crazy out of her mouth," Michelle mumbled.

"I'll try." Sasha smirked.

"Well, look who's here," Carla said. "What brings ya'll down here on this beautiful day?"

Sasha didn't reply; she just rolled her eyes and continued eating her food. Michelle felt the bad vibe and tried to ease the tension a little.

"We just came to pick up my new phone and grab something to eat before heading home."

Carla sat down in one of the empty seats, then took off her sunglasses. "You mind if I join you for a while?"

"You're already sitting there, aren't you?" Sasha replied sarcastically while taking a sip of her drink.

46

Carla never even responded to her. Instead, she just sparked a conversation with Michelle. Carla was unscathed by anything Sasha had to say. The real reason Sasha didn't like her was because one day when she wasn't home, Marcus had gone over to Carla's house to see her husband. When Carla answered the door, she only had on a bikini because she was in the sauna.

One of Sasha's cousins was on her way to see Sasha and had seen her husband standing there talking to Carla. The cousin thought Sasha's husband was having an affair, and that caused a bit of hatred between the two, even though Sasha later found out it wasn't true. The real reason Sasha didn't like Carla was the fact that Carla thought her shit didn't stink.

"Well, actually, we were just about to leave. I have to get home before my son gets there. He's coming home from college today with his girlfriend," Sasha said proudly.

With that said, they got up to leave, leaving Carla still sitting there. She watched them walk away, thinking about how she would get back at Sasha for playing her again.

* * *

"With just under ten seconds left on the clock, Kevin Green steps up to the foul line, trying to tie the game to force the Wizards into overtime," the announcer said over the PA system.

He took a deep breath, bent his knees, bounced the ball a couple of times, and shot. The ball hit the backboard, then dropped through the net. Kevin took a step back as his teammates patted him on the back, giving him encouragement to make the next shot.

"Time out," one of the players told the ref.

They all walked over to the coach so he could design a play for after the next shot. Kevin and Marcus were both placed on the trading block earlier in the month, but so far there were no takers. The GM of the Sixers was trying to free up some salary cap space. He figured with Kevin and Marcus taking up half of that space, they would be able to get a few younger players and still have room for a premier player.

"Okay, this is what I want you to do after Kev makes the free throw. Go zone, and don't let them get past half court, and most importantly, don't foul," the coach said. "Let's get this game into overtime, and then we can go for the win."

The officials blew the whistle, signaling that the timeout was over, and the teams went back out on the floor. Kevin took his place back on the foul line, preparing for his next shot that would hopefully send them into OT. He looked at Marcus, who gave him a wink and head nod, then took the ball from the ref.

The crowd got really loud, trying to distract him so that he'd miss the basket. Kevin shot the ball, and just as it looked like it was about to go in, it bounced off the rim. Out of nowhere, Marcus leaped into the air, grabbed the ball, and slammed it through the rim. Everyone was silent as the Wizards called a timeout. The announcers went crazy.

There were now only eight seconds on the clock, and now Washington was out of timeouts as well. What no one knew was Marcus and Kevin had planned that shot. If it didn't work, it would have looked like he just missed it, but it did work. Now Marcus was the star that had momentarily won the game for them.

"Okay, now let's get a stop here. No fouls, I repeat, no fouls," the coach said, because they didn't want the other team to go to the line and win.

The player inbounded the ball to John Wall of the Wizards, and he saw a lane straight to the rim. He took off, with the guard from the Sixers chasing him. Just as he went to lay up the ball, Kevin came out of nowhere and blocked the shot, sending the ball into the stands. The buzzer went off, ending the game, and the Sixers won 97–96.

"We won, man. Now we're only two games out of the playoffs," Kev said as they walked out of the stadium toward the team bus.

"Don't worry, bro. We just have to keep playing and control our own destiny," replied Marcus. "Now let's go grab those chicks that was checking us out at the hotel yesterday, and take them back to the room."

"Naw, you go ahead and have fun. I'm just gonna get some rest and call Michelle to make sure she's okay," Kev said, trying to relax in the seat.

"Suit yourself. That's more fun for me," Marcus said, calling the girls to meet him in the lobby.

After arriving back at the hotel, everyone went their separate ways. Kev went to his room, took a hot bath, then called his wife. He didn't get an answer, which he found strange considering that she always waited on his call after a game. He figured she probably fell asleep, and decided to just leave her a message.

"Hey, baby, it's me. I hope you saw the end of the game and how me and Marcus won it for us. Just call me as soon as you wake up. It doesn't matter what time it is. I love you," he said before ending the call.

He decided to go down to the bar area to get a couple of drinks before going to sleep. As he stepped onto the elevator, a beautiful female was about to step off. She had on a bikini top with shorts. She and the singer Shakira could pass as identical twins. Kevin just watched as she smiled and exited the elevator. He stared until the doors were shut.

"Damn, she was bad. I need to see my baby soon, or I might do something crazy," he said to himself.

* * *

Marcus was in his suite with the two females he had called earlier. They were sitting in the Jacuzzi, drinking the night away. One of the girls began to come out of her top, then threw it on Marcus's head. They all started laughing while the other girl did the same. The two females started making out in front of Marcus, causing him to get an erection.

After a couple of minutes of girl-on-girl action, Marcus decided to get in on the action. Marcus and one of the girls started tongue kissing, while the other one started massaging his penis, causing it to jump with each stroke. She went under the water and took him into her mouth. You could tell she was a pro, because she didn't come up for air for a couple of minutes.

"Eat this pussy, baby," the girl said, wrapping her legs around his shoulders, with her pussy lips inches away from his mouth.

Marcus grabbed her ass cheeks, stuck his tongue out, and slowly licked and sucked on her clitoris. She came instantly from being tongue fucked.

"Oh, yes, right there, baby. That's my spot," she squealed. Her eyes rolled in the back of her head.

"Let's take this to the bed," Marcus said, feeling his own orgasm getting near from the bone-crushing blowjob the other girl was giving him.

The trio eagerly exited the hot tub and went over to the bed. The girls were really horny now from all the foreplay. The only thing that could satisfy them now was something long and hard inside each of their walls.

Marcus was the first to set things in motion. He pushed both girls onto the king-size bed, then stood over them. The girl with the blond hair eased her way to the edge, giving Marcus a view of her pink tunnel. He put on a condom and leveled his penis right over her moist pussy. He began rubbing it up and down her slit, making her squirm with anticipation. Tired of teasing her, he entered inside and damn near came instantly from the wetness and warmth.

While he was fucking the blonde, the other girl was sitting on her face. Marcus grabbed the other girl's hair roughly and started kissing her as he continued to pound away. After a few more strokes, he pulled out then checked the condom, making sure it was still intact.

"Come bring that chocolate ass over here," he stated, helping the girl off the bed.

The blonde white girl scooted back, giving the other girl some space to lean over. She bent over on the bed and spread her legs open so Marcus could fuck her doggy style.

"What are you waiting for, baby? Take what's yours," she replied in a seductive voice.

Marcus spread her ass cheeks and slid right on in. She arched her back and made a clapping noise around his dick. The girl was meeting him thrust for thrust, enjoying every moment of it. Marcus thought he was in heaven, when he looked down and saw the white girl between his legs, licking and sucking on his balls. Each time she released them, they would make a popping noise. That ceased when she tried to stick a finger in his ass. He jumped and almost smacked the girl.

"What are you doing? I don't down like that," he said, putting his dick back inside of the black girl. "Matter of fact, get over here, so I can teach you a lesson."

The girl got up off the floor, then got back on the bed. Marcus ordered her to get on top of the other girl, with her ass in the air as well. He took turns with each woman until he couldn't control it any longer. Just as he was about to shoot his load, the room door opened.

"Oh my God," Sasha screamed, watching her husband and the two ladies sprawled out on the bed.

Marcus jumped at the sound of Sasha's voice, and so did the girls. They didn't know who Sasha was, but they knew something bad was about to happen. Sasha picked up the first thing she saw, which was a glass on the table, and threw it at Marcus. He ducked just in time and grabbed the robe on the chair. Sasha turned around and stormed out the door.

"Sasha, wait," Marcus yelled, chasing her out into the hallway. He caught up to her before she reached the elevator. "Baby, please let me explain."

She turned around and swung on him, barely missing his jaw. "What the hell do you need to explain?" I caught you in bed with not one, but *two* girls, and you want to explain what to me? Let me guess, it's not what it looks like, right?" she stated, being sarcastic.

"Baby, please calm down. I got drunk after the game and didn't know what I was doing," Marcus said.

"Out of all the lies you could have probably gotten away with, you picked that one. I don't want to hear anything you have to say, and I sure as hell don't want to be in your presence right now. I'm going home, and tomorrow, you can best believe that my lawyer will be drawing up our divorce papers," Sasha said before letting the elevator door shut in Marcus's face.

He didn't even try to stop her, because he was caught red-handed. He rushed back to his room and closed the door. The girls were both sitting on the bed, dressed and ready to leave. Marcus walked over to the bed, and to the girls' surprise, took off his robe and stood there buck naked.

"Who told y'all to get dressed? We haven't finished yet, so come up out of those clothes."

The girls looked at each other and smiled. They stayed with him for the rest of the night, taking turns pleasing each other. Marcus didn't even care about his marriage right now. The only thing that was on his mind was the two beauties that were in his bed, and the cocaine on the table.

Four

Michelle was inside Kevin's hotel room looking for him. She noticed that his room hadn't been touched at all, except for when he left for his game. This gave her time to get ready, so she sat down on the bed. She looked at her cell phone and noticed that he had called a couple of times. Michelle was about to call back, when her phone started ringing. It was Sasha, so she answered. "Hey, girl!" she said, lying back on the bed.

She didn't get a response. Instead, she heard Sasha sobbing on the other end of the phone.

"Sasha, what's wrong? Talk to me girl. Where are you at?" Michelle said, starting to worry.

"I caught my husband having an affair. He was in the bed with two women when I walked in," she said, crying.

"Where are you at right now, so I can come there."

"In the lobby," Sasha replied.

Michelle grabbed her purse, then ran out the door. She said to herself that she would call Kevin after she checked on her best friend. The elevator was taking too long, so she took the stairs.

When she reached the lobby, Sasha was sitting at the bar having a drink. Michelle walked over and sat next to her on the stool. Sasha put her head on Michelle's shoulders and cried.

"It's okay. Tell me everything that happened?" Michelle said, rubbing her hair.

"Well, it's simple, I wanted to surprise him tonight, but I ended up being the one surprised. I'm telling you, Chelle, if I had my gun, I would have committed murder tonight," Sasha said, downing the drink she got from the bartender. "Fill it up again, please."

"You need to take it easy, girl, with these drinks. I'm going to call Kevin and see where he is," Michelle said, dialing his number. She finally got an answer after trying twice.

"Hey, I tried to call you after my game, but ya didn't answer," Kevin stated.

"I'm in your hotel lobby at the bar with Sasha. She caught Marcus with his pants down. Literally! Where are you at?"

"I'm in the lobby at the bar too. I don't see you," he said, looking around for his wife. He spotted her on the other side. "Here I come now. I see y'all."

When Michelle saw him walking toward them, she disconnected the call. She got up and greeted him with a passionate kiss. Not trying to impede on their moment, Sasha turned her head and signaled for the bartender to bring her another drink. She was feeling tipsy now, and these images started spiraling out of control. Sasha thought the drinks would make it go away, but instead, it only enhanced her imagination even more.

After Michelle told Kevin what had happened, he went over to Sasha and gave her a hug.

"I'm gonna have a long talk with him, okay? Let Chelle take you up to my room. Y'all can stay in there tonight, and I'll take you home in the morning," Kevin said.

Kevin was really feeling guilty because he knew what his friend was doing upstairs. He too would have been caught up if he had accepted Marcus's offer earlier. Fortunately, he didn't, and he had to play the advocate right now.

"I'm okay. I just want to have a few more drinks. Why don't you two go back to your room and celebrate y'all's victory," Sasha said, slurring her words.

"No, we can celebrate another time. Right now, we're going to get you out of here before you end up doing something crazy."

They all headed back up to Kevin's suite. After making sure they were okay, Kevin headed over to Marcus's suite.

He knocked on the door four times before someone answered. As soon as Marcus opened the door, Kevin shook his head.

"Man, are you stupid or what?"

"What are you talking about?" Marcus replied, walking back over toward the bed where the two sleeping beauties were lying.

"That right there is what I'm talking about," Kevin said, grabbing him and turning him around. "Your wife is in my room with Chelle, crying her heart out, and you're still in here with these two hos."

"I'm not trying to hear that shit right now. She said she wants a divorce. I might as well enjoy myself. Besides, tomorrow I will just buy her something expensive," he stated.

Kevin could see that Marcus's eyes were open wider than usual, and when he looked at his nose, it was red. That's when it hit him that his friend was using again.

"I know you're not snorting that shit again. Man, you need some serious help. Get rid of them," he said, pointing at the girls, "by tomorrow morning before your wife, that you've been married to for eighteen years, gets up." Then he turned and walked out the door, leaving Marcus looking stupid.

* * *

The next morning, just as she said, Sasha called her lawyer about filing the paperwork for a divorce. He suggested that they go to marriage counseling first, before she made any rash decisions. At first, she wasn't trying to hear any of that, but better heads prevailed, and she took his advice. The real reason was she was still in love with him despite all his flaws.

"Knock, knock, knock." There was someone knocking at the door. When she opened it up, Marcus was standing there with a bouquet of flowers and a rectangular box that was gift-wrapped.

"May I come in so we can talk?" he asked, staring at her.

"For what, Marcus? You finally left your little skanks at the hotel, and now you want to make up with me? Well, I really don't want to hear any of it, so take your flowers and gifts and go to hell back where you came from," Sasha replied, walking away from the door.

Since she didn't try to shut it in his face, Marcus took that as a sign that she really wanted him to come in. He closed the door and walked into the living room, where Sasha was sitting on the couch. He sat next to her, then placed a hand over hers.

"Baby, I made a mistake, and I'm willing to spend the rest of my life trying to fix it. I know you can't forgive me right now, but can ya please give me one chance to make things right between us?"

Sasha pulled her hand away and turned her head as tears fell from her eyes.

"My lawyer wants us to go to counseling starting Monday morning, so make sure you're there, or you'll be sorry. Until we settle our differences, the guest room is all yours," she stated firmly. She stood up and headed toward the stairs. "I'm going shopping, so do what you want?"

Grateful for another chance, Marcus got up and went over to the bar to pour himself a drink. He was still in the doghouse, but knew with time, all wounds would heal.

Marcus called Kevin to tell him what had gone down.

"Hello," Kevin answered.

"Everything is okay, man. We are going to marriage counseling on Monday. She's still pissed off, but after tonight she will be all over me again," Marcus said, thinking about the new Mercedes that he got for her.

"I don't know about that, dawg. She is not just going to forget about what she saw last night. I think you need to give it some time and give her some space. Let her be the one who makes the first move, or you will be in even deeper shit," Kev said.

Marcus thought about what his friend was saying for a minute, before responding, "You're right, man. I'm just going to take it slow and see where it leads. I just don't want her to get a divorce, because it will be a nasty one."

70

"Trust me, I know. She caught your stupid ass red-handed." Kev smirked. "Seriously, you stand to lose everything if that happens, and that greedy bitch lawyer she has will have your wife living on an island somewhere."

"I know, I know. I don't even want to think about that right now. How about we get to practice before we're late?" Marcus said, grabbing his car keys off the table.

"We will talk more about this afterward 'cause I'm not trying to have my wife thinking negatively about me too. I know how to be discrete, but you, you just do your dirt out in the open for everyone to see. Now let me tell you about this shorty I ran into when I got a drink last night. She was . . ." Kev said as he walked out the door.

Morgan and one of his colleagues were exiting the building after a long and boring meeting, when he noticed an envelope on the window of his car.

"See you tomorrow, Morgan, and don't forget that we'll be heading to city hall to discuss hosting the Democratic Convention," Doug said, starting his car up.

"I'll be ready," Morgan replied picking up the envelope before getting inside his car.

There was no return address on it, so he didn't know where or whom it had come from. When he opened it up, there was a note and a DVD inside. He opened up the note first and read it.

Dear Mr. Wright,

I know you're wondering what this is all about. Well, it's simple. I know all about you and your secretary. If you don't believe me, then watch the DVD. I want 50 grand by next Friday, or I'll send it to your wife. I'll be in touch with the time and location. Good day, sir!

~ A friend

Morgan quickly inserted the video into his car stereo. When he pressed play, he felt a sense of déjà vu come over him as he watched himself and his secretary having sex in the hotel room. He watched the whole video, then ejected the DVD and broke it in half. Morgan sat there in silence trying to figure out who was blackmailing him and how they were able to get that footage. First he thought that Symira had something to do with it, but if she did, who was with her. He decided to give her a call.

"Hello, Mr. Wright, is everything okay?" Symira answered after three rings.

Morgan knew by her calling him by his last name that she was with her husband or she couldn't talk right now.

"Hi, Symira. I need you to go somewhere private real quick so I can ask you something."

74

"I'll check the messages now and call you right back, sir," she said before ending the call.

A couple of minutes later, she called him back. He didn't waste any time trying to get to the bottom of this.

"Who did you have recording us at the hotel?" he stated with anger in his voice.

"What? What do you mean by that?" she replied, trying to figure out what he was talking about.

"Someone recorded us the other night, and now they are trying to scam me out of fifty grand. You wouldn't know anything about that would you?"

Symira was livid. "Are you suggesting that I would try to use you for fifty grand? I don't know anything about that, and you are a jerk for even thinking I had something to do with it," Symira told him.

"I'm sorry for accusing you of something like that. Somebody saw us, though, and now I have to pay them by next Friday or they are going to send the video to my wife. Look at what our indiscretions have cost us. I'm surprised they are not trying to get something out of you too," Morgan said, trying to figure out what's going on.

"I really don't know how they saw us. Did they even leave a name or anything?"

"No, it just said, 'from a friend.' Man, what the hell am I going to do? What if I pay them the money and they still send that shit to my wife? I would be in a messy situation. This divorce would cost me everything," Morgan stated.

"We will talk about it tomorrow morning before the meeting. That will give us time to clear our heads and figure out who could be behind this," Symira replied.

"Alright, meet me there at seven. That way we'll have a couple of hours to figure this shit out," he said. "Until then, though, we can't be sneaking around anymore. Your husband will kill both of us if he finds out about us."

Symira's husband was a professional kickboxer, and he had just returned from a championship match in Atlantic City. He lost his belt to someone who had only eight wins, which made him bitter. Before that fight he was undefeated. His coach and trainers knew he wasn't ready, but he insisted on fighting anyway. He ended up tapping out in the second round.

Symira ended the call and went into the bedroom with her husband. She lay on the bed, and for the next few minutes, she tried to figure out who was behind the whole thing. She didn't have any enemies, so it was hard to figure out. She fell asleep dreaming about what life would be like without her husband in it.

* * *

By the time Morgan arrived at his office, Symira was already searching the office. He sat his briefcase down on the desk, then looked in her direction.

"What are you doing?" he asked.

"Checking to see if there's any hidden cameras in here. Somebody has been watching us, and we need to find out who," Symira replied, standing on the foot ladder, looking into the vent.

"There's nothing here. They took the video at the hotel, not in the office. Security wouldn't let them in my office without my prior permission."

Symira sighed as she stepped off the ladder. She walked over to where Morgan was now sitting, and sat on his lap. He rubbed her back with one hand while unbuttoning her blouse with the other. He grabbed one of her titties out of her bra and began fondling it. She closed her eyes, trying to enjoy the moment, but was suddenly interrupted by the sound of the elevator door opening. They hurried up and fixed their clothes like nothing had happened.

"They are here early," Morgan whispered, looking at the people walking toward their desks. We'll finish this some other time, but right now I have a meeting to get ready for. Cancel all my appointments for tomorrow, and we will spend it trying to find out who is blackmailing us."

"Okay, I'll think of something to tell my husband, but we have to be careful from now on. I hope we win the bid because it will surely bring a lot of money to this city if we

79

can host it," Symira said, sitting down in front of her computer.

"Me too!" Morgan replied, heading into the conference room so they could go over everything before heading to city hall.

Six

Marcus came home around noon because he wanted to give his wife the key to her new car. When he walked into the house, he heard someone in the kitchen cooking. He eased his way toward the kitchen and was surprised at what he saw. His son's girlfriend was standing over the stove cooking, with nothing on but her panties and a T-shirt.

Marcus stood there admiring her frame for a couple of minutes. Her French-cut panties were so tight that they barely covered any part of her butt. They almost looked like thongs from the way they fit. Marcus was about to walk away, but his feet wouldn't move, as if he was nailed to the floor. Akiylah turned around and dropped her plate to the floor from being so frightened by him standing there.

"Oh my God, me sorry. You startled me," she said, bending down to pick up the broken glass.

"I'm sorry, I thought you were my wife. Let me help you get that up," he replied, walking over in her direction.

"Me can get it, sir. It's no problem."

Marcus noticed her Caribbean accent. He wondered what island she was from. His eyes were glued to the bush that was sticking out from her panties as she kneeled down

82

putting the glass in a trash bag. She noticed what he was staring at and immediately felt embarrassed.

"Me sorry that me not dressed. Me just wanted to make some breakfast. Me go put clothes on now," she said, getting up to go upstairs to put something on.

"It's okay. I too sometimes walk around in my boxers and wifebeater. Just finish what you're doing. I'm going into the living room to watch TV," he said, easing the tension between them. "Where is my son at?"

"He went with his friend to the gym. They left a few minutes ago," Akiylah said.

"If you don't mind me asking, where are you from?" Marcus said, standing in the doorway.

"Me from the Virgin Islands. Me came here to see your son and maybe get married."

Marcus was shocked that his son had gone and gotten a mail-order wife. Then an idea came into his head. He wanted to see if she was truly worthy of marrying his son.

"Well, around here, in order for me to let my son marry you, you have to prove your loyalty," he stated, coming back over to where she was now standing.

"How do me do that?" she stated.

"Come here and I'll show you," Marcus said, sitting on the chair.

Akiylah walked over to Marcus and stood in front of him. He pulled her onto his lap and palmed her butt. She didn't know what to do, so she just went along with it. He then lifted her shirt up, exposing her perky breast. Marcus began sucking on her nipples one at a time until they became as hard as pebbles. Akiylah tried to resist his touch,

84

but the heat from her pussy made it impossible. She let out a soft moan in her native accent, which made Marcus suck harder.

She began to dry hump on the bulge coming from the shorts he was wearing. Akiylah pulled her shirt all the way over her head, exposing her mocha-chocolate frame. Her body was so flawless that you couldn't even find a mark on it. Marcus didn't even regret the fact that he was about to have sex with his son's girlfriend. He was letting the head between his legs do all the thinking for him. He had somehow manipulated her into surrendering her body to him.

Marcus undid the string on his shorts, pulled them down enough to free his manhood. He lifted her body slightly, just enough to position her vagina over his erection. He pulled her panties to the side, and that's when

85

Akiylah took over, because now she was so horny that she could have fucked the banana sitting in the fruit bowl. She placed his dick at her entrance and sat down on it.

"Mmmmm," was all she could say as she began pumping up and down while holding onto his neck slightly.

Marcus was so into it now that any doubts he once had had faded with his morals. He gripped her ass, spreading her pussy open, and started pumping faster, matching each stroke.

"Me loving having sex. You feel so good, I don't want you to stop," she said as she started whining uncontrollably. Every stroke sent shock waves throughout her body. Marcus was on the brink of an orgasm within the next two minutes.

"Wow, girl, I'm about to cum," he said, slowing down, trying to avoid the inevitable.

"Not yet, me not ready yet," she replied, breathing hard.

Akiylah started working her body, trying to get hers before he got his.

Just as she was about to cum, Marcus pulled out and came all over the floor. Akiylah just watched him until he was done. She then got up off his lap and lay on the table, spreading her legs and giving him a full view of her love tunnel.

"It's me turn to cum, daddy, so handle your business," she said as she started rubbing her clit.

Marcus wasn't with eating pussy right now, but the sight of her hairy mound enticed him. He pulled the chair up toward the table and buried his face in her bushy hole. He licked, then sucked on her clit until her body started shaking. As she came, Marcus began to blow into her pussy. That sensation sent her over the edge.

"I don't know if you're ready for my son to settle down with," Marcus said, fixing his clothes.

Akiylah got off the table and grabbed her shirt off the floor. After she put it on, she looked at Marcus with pleading eyes.

"Was me not good enough just now? What did me do wrong? Me promise to do better."

She started to cry because she thought that she didn't live up to his expectations. Marcus wanted to bust out laughing, but he held it in. He decided to play this opportunity for what it was worth.

"Don't cry. I was just playing with you," he said patting her back. "I would love for you to be a part of this family, as long as we can spend some time together once in a while."

Akiylah really wanted to stay here with Marcus's son, so she agreed to his demands. Besides that, she knew that she had just betrayed her man by sleeping with his father, so now she had to do what he said or lose any chance she had of staying here. What she didn't want to do was go back to being poor.

Marcus went upstairs to take a quick shower before he went to meet up with Kev. The thought of his wife or son coming in never even crossed his mind. He now had an in-house jump-off that was at his disposal, and as long as she kept her mouth closed, he was good. Nobody would ever know about his deception, or so he thought.

* * *

Carla and Rapheal continued to have their piano lessons twice a week. There were times when they even flirted with each other, but it never led to anything but just that. Her husband had so much going on at work that she hadn't heard from him or slept with him in four days. To make matters worse, they were supposed to be organizing a baby shower. Carla had been trying to handle it for the past two days, and when she called, his secretary always said he was too busy. She decided to take care of it herself. She called and arranged everything, then sent out all the invitations. When she ended the last call, Rapheal came in and sat next to her. He passed her a cup of coffee.

"Thank you," she said taking a sip. "Mmmm, this is good. Is it the expensive stuff?"

"Nothing but the best for my customers. I figured since y'all pay so much for lessons, I might as well treat everyone once in a while," he replied.

"Awww, such a charmer."

"Is it working?" he stated.

"Maybe, if I wasn't wearing this," she smiled, holding her hand up so he could see her wedding band.

He just smiled and stood up. He walked over and sat down at the piano.

"So today I thought I would teach you that John Legend song, "All of Me." It's a very easy piece, and I know you will pick up on it with no problem because you are a fast learner," Rapheal said as he began to play the song.

"All of me, loves all of you. Love your curves and all your edges, all your perfect imperfections. Give your all to me, I'll give my all to you. You're my end and my

91

beginning, even when I lose, I'm winning," he sang while playing the beautiful melody.

Carla listened to his voice and couldn't help getting turned on by the words. That song had a lot of meaning to it. She thought that he was singing it to her.

"'Cause I give you all of me, and you give me all of you," he continued to sing until he went through the whole song.

"Now, I want you to play these chords first to get warmed up. Then we will go from there," Rapheal said, playing a few chords.

Carla listened to the notes again and watched his hands. As much as she tried to concentrate, she couldn't. She needed to see her husband before she did something out of character.

"I have to leave now. There's something that I need to do today. I'll pay you for the whole session, but this can't wait," she said, putting her jacket on.

"Is everything okay?" he said.

"Yes, everything is fine. I just forgot to turn the oven off, and nobody is home," Carla answered, running out the door.

Rapheal ran to the door just as she was opening her car door.

"If you want a makeup session, just call me, and I'll set it up."

"Okay, thanks. See you later," Carla said. She started the car and pulled off. When she got around the corner from the center, she pulled over to get her bearings. The pregnancy always had her horny.

She leaned back on the headrest and closed her eyes. Her hand mysteriously found its way to the button on her jeans. She opened her jeans and stuck her hand inside, rubbing on her silk panties. Carla's car had a very dark tint on it, so no one could see who was inside unless they were up on the window.

John Legend's song came on the radio, and she thought back to when Rapheal was playing it on the piano. That made her move her fingers against her panties even harder. She became so wet that it started seeping through, causing her fingers to become moist. Carla stuck her hand into her mouth, tasting her own juices, then began fingering her pussy. Just as she was building up to cum, someone tapped on the window, causing her to jump in her seat. When she looked up, it was the parking authority officer. Carla fixed her clothes and rolled the window down.

"Yes," she said, trying not to give away what she was doing.

"Ma'am, you have to move your car. This is a bus stop, and the bus won't be able to pull over with you sitting here," the officer said.

"Oh, I'm sorry! I'll move right now."

"Thank you and enjoy the rest of your day," the officer said.

Carla pulled off into traffic. She decided to pay her husband an unexpected visit. She smiled at the thought of what she was about to do. She was going to fuck her husband in his office, on his desk. It just couldn't wait any longer. Her pussy was throbbing, and it needed to be tamed.

Twenty minutes later, she was in the elevator, on her way up to Morgan's office. When she stepped off the elevator, it was too quiet. She walked into his office to find it empty. She took out her cell phone to call him and see where he was at. While she was dialing his number, Symira walked out of the bathroom.

"Oh, hi, Mrs. Wright. Are you looking for your husband?" Symira asked.

"Yes, is he around?"

"No, but he'll be back in a few hours. He had to go meet with a very important colleague," Symira said, not trying to tell her whom he really had gone to see.

"Oh, I wanted to surprise him, but he's not here. Just tell him that I came by and that I'll see him when he gets home," Carla said, heading for the door.

"You sure there's nothing I can do for you?" Symira replied, walking over toward her. "I can smell the fragrance coming from your vagina. Not to mention the wet spot on your jeans."

Carla looked down, noticing that the front of her jeans were wet from the pre-climax she had earlier. She felt embarrassed as she tried to cover them up.

"Don't be embarrassed. Your secret is safe with me," she whispered into her ear. "Take those pants off and give them to me so I can dry them before you leave."

"That's okay. They'll be dry by the time I get home," Carla stated firmly.

She could tell by the way Symira was looking at her that her intentions were not good at all. She could feel her undressing her with her eyes. Carla opened the door and walked out. Before she shut it, she said, "The next time you look at me that way, I'll tell my husband to fire you."

Symira smiled as Carla closed the door behind her. Symira knew that Morgan would never fire her, so she laughed it off and went back to work.

"Feisty, just like I like them," she said to no one in particular.

Carla headed home to take a shower and fix dinner before Morgan got home. She also called her son to tell him to take out some meat for her. She blasted the car stereo all the way home, enjoying the breeze.

$\mathcal{S}$even

Morgan pulled up to the coffee shop to wait for further instructions. The person that was blackmailing him had contacted him about an hour ago and told him to meet him with the money or else his wife would receive a very special piece of mail.

He stepped out of the car, then walked over and sat at one of the outside tables. Morgan had the manila envelope in his jacket pocket, and his 9 mm pistol was tucked safely in the small of his back. He kept looking around at every face that passed him, wondering who would stop and confront him. A couple of minutes later, Morgan heard his phone ringing. He pulled it out to check the caller ID, but it wasn't his phone. It kept ringing, so he looked around until he found it taped under the table. He snatched it and hit the accept button.

"Hello," he said.

"You got my money? Because I really don't have time for games," responded the caller.

"Yes, I have your money. Now come show your face so I can see who the hell I'm dealing with."

"In time, my friend. Right now I need you to take that phone with you and get into your car. I hope you didn't call the police or have someone follow you, or you'll be sorry," the caller said.

"I'm here alone, so where do you want me to go?" Morgan asked as he got into his car.

"Just drive north until I tell you to stop. You'll then place the money into the mailbox of my choice, hop back into your car, and go ahead with your life without me," the caller said.

Morgan did exactly as he was told, and within a half hour, he had dropped the money and was on his way home. Just as he was pulling into his driveway, the cell phone rang again.

"What is it now? I've done everything you told me to. Now stay out of my life," he screamed into the phone.

"Morgan, I was just sitting here thinking. Since you gave away fifty grand so easy, maybe it wouldn't hurt you to give away another fifty?"

"What are you talking about? You said it was over, and now you're trying to get more money out of me. Are you crazy?" Morgan replied.

"Before you ask me if I'm crazy, why don't you go to the video on the phone I gave you. I'm quite sure you'll have a change of heart afterward," the caller said, then hung up.

Morgan pulled up the video called "Morgan," then to his surprise, he found himself the center of yet another sex tape. There he was, with Symira bent over the desk at his office. It felt like a stream of blood rushed to his head. This was deeper than he thought. Someone was watching all his deceptions. He felt like he was on the show *Cheaters*. The cell phone rang again.

"Do I have your attention now?"

"Why are you doing this? Is this some type of game you're playing, spying on me?" he asked.

"See, the problem is, you're too cocky about everything. You think that just because you're the governor's assistant, you can do what you want. I'm tired of people like you, so you will do what I say or suffer the consequences of your actions," the caller said with authority.

"I need time to get that kind of money again. You'll have to give me a couple of weeks," Morgan replied, feeling defeated.

"I'll be in touch. Don't lose the phone 'cause it's the only number I'm going to call. Enjoy the rest of your day Mr. Wright," he said, then ended the call.

Morgan looked at the phone, then threw it in the glove compartment. He knew he had to formulate a plan, because there was no way he was going to keep getting extorted. He needed to use all his connections to take care of this problem, and that's what he planned on doing.

* * *

Kevin pulled up in front of the post office to drop off the packages his wife gave him. When he walked in, he noticed a familiar face standing at the counter. It was the same lady from a week ago in the elevator. She was looking even more beautiful than she did the last time he'd seen her. He wondered what she was doing in Philadelphia, because when he saw her, it was in Washington. Kevin decided to say something to her, even if it was just a flirt. As he got closer, he noticed her Spanish accent and decided to play off of it.

"*Me permite*? (Would you let me?)" he said, walking up to the counter with his credit card in hand.

She turned around and looked to see whom it was. Once she saw Kevin, a smile came across her face.

"*Si, iadelante*! (Yes, go ahead!)" she replied.

After he paid for the shipment of both of their packages, they walked outside into the parking lot. Kevin began to spark up a conversation just so she wouldn't leave so soon.

"*Buenas tardes. Me llamo* Kevin (Good afternoon. My name is Kevin)," he said holding out his hand.

105

"*Mucho gusto, senor* Kevin (A pleasure, sir Kevin)."

"*Y lo que te llamo?* (And what do I call you?)," he said, kissing the back of her hand.

She blushed momentarily, before pulling her hand back. At first she didn't say anything. Then she answered his question.

"*Me llamo Seleena* (My name is Seleena)," she said, running her fingers through her hair.

"*Mucho gusto* (A pleasure)," Kevin said with a smile.

He walked her to her car and opened the door. She stepped inside, and Kevin closed it. After she started it up, she rolled the window down.

"*Yo no sabia que tu sabes hablar Espanol* (I did not know that you know speak Spanish)," Seleena said.

"*Hay mucho de mí que no sabes* (There is much about me you don't know)."

106

Seleena was impressed at how fluently he spoke Spanish. She thought that he was half-and-half. Kevin knew what she was thinking, and answered the question for her.

"No, I just took Spanish as a second language in high school. Both of my parents were mixed, though."

"Okay. I'm 100 percent Spanish. I came here from Puerto Rico when I was only one year old," she said.

"We need to talk some more. *Quieres ir a comer?* (Would you like to go out to eat?)" he said with pleading eyes.

"*Acepto la oferta* (I accept the offer)," Seleena replied, giving him a card with her number on it.

"I'll pick you up at seven. Before you go, why are you out here? I seen you in Washington, DC," Kevin said.

"Yeah, my friend plays for the Wizards. I was mad when you missed that free throw and your teammate dunked it to win the game," she replied.

"I see you know a little about the game. That gives us a lot to talk about tonight. Just make sure your ready when I get there," Kevin said walking toward his car.

"I'll be ready. See you later," Seleena told him. Then she pulled off, leaving him with a big smile on his face.

Kevin drove home trying to figure out what he was going to tell his wife. He knew it was just infatuation that made him want to spend time with her, but as long as he didn't get caught, he didn't care.

When he got home, his son was sitting on the steps with his iPad. Mike was the spitting image of Kevin. The only difference between the two was their ages, and you couldn't hardly tell that either.

"What's good, Pop?" Mike said, sitting the iPad down and giving his dad a half hug.

"Sit, did your mom get back from the gallery?" he asked, sitting on the steps next to Mike.

"Naw, she said she was going to stop and see Grandma before she comes home. She said that we can order out tonight 'cause she's not cooking, just save her some."

"Well, I'm about to take a shower so I can meet with an advertising agent. What are you doing today?"

"Nothing, I'm just going to stay home and watch TV or play Xbox until I hear from this girl I met the other day," Mike replied.

"Oh, just make sure you strap up," Kevin stated, winking at his son.

"For sure, Pops. You know how I do."

Kevin went inside, leaving Mike outside. Mike went back on Instagram to finish checking out the latest news on different celebrities, when he saw Sasha pull up. She got out of the car wearing a tennis skirt and jacket. Mike smiled and waved to her.

"Hey, Mike, have you seen my lazy son? I want him to help me with these groceries," Sasha said.

"No, I haven't seen him all day. I'll give you a hand," Mike stated, walking over toward her.

"Thank you so much. That is very nice of you. If you like, you can join us for dinner tonight."

"Since my mom don't want to cook, that would be nice. What are you making?" Mike asked, grabbing the bags of groceries out of the back seat.

"I'm not sure yet. I was going to either make some fish or some meatloaf."

"Either one of them will be good. I'll let my dad know that he will be eating alone tonight," he said with a smile.

"We'll just send a plate over after it's done," Sasha replied, opening the door.

Mike took the bags in and sat them on the kitchen counter. When he walked back into the living room, Sasha was taking off her shoes. He went over and stood by the ottoman. Sasha picked up the shoes, then headed upstairs.

"I'm going to change my clothes. You can watch TV or come back in an hour. Dinner should be ready by then."

Mike watched her walk up the steps. She had on a thong, so he could see her ass cheeks sticking out. He licked his lips as he walked out the door, thinking about seeing her naked. Mike had to admit that Sasha's body was definitely in wonderful shape. He even wondered how many times Sahmeer may have been looking at his mom in the same way. He shook the thought from his mind and went back to his house.

An hour went past. Then Mike went over to Sasha's house for dinner. Marcus wasn't home yet, but Sahmeer was. They sat down and ate their food while talking about little things. Sasha had set a plate of food to the side for her husband and Mike's dad.

"That was delicious. Thank you so much, Mrs. Sasha," Mike stated, wiping his mouth with a napkin.

"Would you like some more?" she asked. "We have plenty left."

"No thanks. I'm stuffed. All I want to do now is go to sleep," he replied.

"Mom, this was really good. I miss coming home to a home-cooked meal. I might have to come home every weekend from now on," Sahmeer said, grabbing his and Akiylah's plate from the table.

"Leave that there. Me and Akiylah will clean up. You boys go do whatever it is that you do," Sasha demanded.

"Thanks, Mom. Thanks, baby," Sahmeer said kissing both of them on the cheek.

"Thanks again, y'all," Mike said again as they walked outside.

"So what do you think about Akiylah? She has really shown me that she will be a loyal chick. I'm going to marry her when I come back home in June," Sahmeer said, sitting in the chair on the porch.

"I think she's cool, but don't you think you're rushing it? I mean, you've only known her for a couple of months now, and June is only two months away. You hardly even know anything about her," Mike replied.

"I know that she's beautiful, and that she came from the Virgin Islands because her family is poor. She won't have to worry about that here, Mike. I will shower her with all the love and gifts to keep her happy. I don't want her to live like that anymore. You feel where I'm coming from."

"I feel you, but I just don't want you to do something that you might regret later," Mike said.

"Thanks for being worried, man," Sahmeer replied, giving his friend a half hug. "My dad even said she's a keeper. He thinks she's very hot."

Mike smiled because he also thought she was hot. He kept glancing at her the whole time they were eating dinner. She was wearing skin-tight jeans and a shirt that made her breasts look perfect.

"So are you trying to watch the game tonight at the sports bar? We can get drunk and walk home," Mike said.

114

"Yeah, that's cool with me. I don't want to go all the way out to West Philly anyway. Our dads are finally in the playoffs. I hope they make it past the first round."

"Don't worry; they're going to take care of business. I'm about to go get dressed, and I'll meet you back here at seven," Mike said, heading back to his house.

"I'll be ready. If I'm not here, it's because I went to take Akiylah to her friend's house. Just stay here with my mom until I get back," Sahmeer told him before going in the house.

Eight

Kevin was at his favorite restaurant with his date Saleena. He didn't have to lie to his wife to get out, because she went to take care of her mom, who was sick with the flu. She was going to be there for a couple of days, so that gave him time to play. They had been having a very good conversation for the last hour while enjoying a very expensive meal.

"*Dime algo sobre tí* (Tell me something about you)," he told Saleena, taking a sip of his wine.

Saleena smiled because she was still impressed at how fluently he spoke Spanish. First impressions meant a lot to her, and right now he had her panties wet. She thought about what her friends used to say when they were growing up in high school: "You'll know if you're going to fuck somebody as soon as you see them."

Saleena knew that if she got him back to her apartment or went to his house, her soaked panties were coming off. She smiled at that thought.

"I told you all about me already. What else do you want to know?" she asked.

"I want to know why you keep squirming in your seat? What's wrong?" Kevin smiled. He thought he knew already why she was doing it. He thought she had to use the restroom.

"You have me horny right now. The whole time that you've been talking to me, you've been fucking my mind. Now I want you to take me somewhere and fuck my body," she replied boldly.

Her boldness surprised Kevin. He wasn't expecting that to come out of her classy mouth. He wasn't going to disappoint her either. Kevin quickly summoned the waitress and paid for their meal. They left the restaurant and only got to the parking garage before they were all over each other.

They started kissing while Kevin squeezed her butt. It was soft and juicy. Saleena pushed him down on top of his Benz, then climbed on top of the hood and stood over top of him.

"Wait, someone might see us," Kevin said, scared that one of his wife's friends might walk past and catch them.

Saleena looked at him seductively and said, "I'll take care of that."

She took off one of her heels and hit all three light bulbs, making the area around them dark. The only way people would know who they were was if they came close to the car. Kevin shook his head as Saleena lifted her skirt up to her waist. All he could see was how fat her pussy lips were through her panties.

"*Por favor se gentil* (Please be gentle)," she said, lowering her body down onto his crotch.

"Don't worry, I'll be gentle," Kevin replied, pulling down his pants.

It was a nice evening, so it wasn't cold out. That wouldn't have stopped him from what he was about to do

119

anyway. He ripped off her panties and leveled his dick with her opening, then pushed her down on it. She let out a scream at first because it hurt. Then the pain subsided and the pleasure kicked in.

"*Solo relajate y dejame encargarme de ti* (Just relax and let me take care of you)," Kevin said as he gently pumped in and out of her soaking wet pussy.

People were exiting the restaurant, but no one noticed the action going on in the corner. Saleena didn't care who saw them. In fact, it was only turning her on even more at the possibility of getting caught. She started pumping even faster as she came all over his dick.

Kevin wanted to get his off now that she got hers. He scooted off the hood of his car, with his dick still inside of her, and held her in the air as he bounced her up and down on it.

He felt his nut building up, and that's when it hit him that he wasn't wearing a condom. He quickly pulled out and squirted all over her stomach, with some getting on her skirt.

"Wow, that was good. Sorry about getting it on your skirt," Kevin said fixing his clothes.

"Don't worry about it, but we have to do this again real soon. I'm free tomorrow. Are you?" she said, putting her panties inside her purse.

"No, I will be on the road preparing for one of the most important games of the season. If we win, we're in the playoffs," Kevin responded, excited.

"I forgot, big basketball star. Well, good luck on your game tomorrow. Call me afterward. I'll have a gift for you to unwrap if you win," she said, giving him a peck on the lips.

He walked her over to her car and shut the door behind her. After watching her pull off, he hopped in his car and headed home. He called his wife and checked on her before retiring for the night. He used the spare key because his was missing.

* * *

It was around three o'clock in the morning when Mike and Sahmeer got home from the bar. Sahmeer was pissy drunk, so Mike let him stay at his house so his mom wouldn't get mad. He helped him over to the couch and took off his shoes.

"Damn, man, you shouldn't be drinking anymore. You can't hold your liquor," Mike stated. "I'll be back. I'm going to go grab some of your clothes from your house."

122

He reached in Sahmeer's pocket and pulled out his house key. Mike would let him wear some of his clothes, but Sahmeer wouldn't be able to fit in them. They wore totally different sizes. Mike walked next door and went up to Sahmeer's room. He grabbed some sweatpants and a shirt and headed down the steps.

Before he reached the bottom, Sasha came out of the room because she heard someone moving around and thought it was Sahmeer.

"Sahmeer, is that you down there?"

Mike turned around and looked up at Sasha standing at the top of the stairs in her nightgown.

"No, Mrs. Sasha. It's me, Mike. I just came over to pick up something for Sahmeer," he said, trying not to let her know that Sahmeer threw up all over his clothes.

"Oh, okay. Tell him that his father will be gone again for another week. He's really getting on my nerves leaving like this," she stated.

Mike was listening to her vent for a couple of minutes, when he heard her start sobbing. He walked up the stairs to make sure she was okay before he went back home. When he walked in her room, she was sitting on the bed, wiping her eyes.

"Are you okay, Mrs. Sasha?" he said, sitting next to her. He couldn't understand what was going on.

She looked up and shook her head. She contemplated telling him what had happened, but didn't know how to say the words.

"I'm just tired of his shit. He runs around doing who knows what, with who knows who, and thinks it's okay.

I'm not going to sit around and wait too much longer," Sasha said, putting her head on Mike's chest.

He put his arm around her and patted her shoulder. Mike knew that Marcus was a dog because he had seen him at lunch with a bad chick before.

"Shhhh, it's okay," he stated, trying to comfort her.

Sasha felt safe for a moment sitting there with him. All of a sudden, Mike felt her hand rubbing his crotch. He jumped up and looked at her. For the first time, he noticed that she was wearing a see-through gown. Her nipples were trying to break out of the fabric. She stood up and walked toward him.

"Don't you think I'm beautiful?" she said, backing him into the wall.

Mike was still tipsy, and it was playing a big part in his thinking process right now. When she touched his dick again, it went straight to attention.

"Mrs. Sasha, I'm friends with your son," he said as she started kissing on his neck.

She unzipped his pants and pulled out his erection. He leaned his head back as she got on her knees and took him into her mouth. All reasoning went out the door when he felt her warm lips all over him. The sensation was driving him crazy. Sasha was impressed at how well-endowed he was. She licked from the head, all way down to his balls, taking them one at a time into her mouth.

Mike felt his orgasm ready to burst out, and started fucking her mouth. Sasha gagged a few times but took every thrust like a professional. When he burst, she swallowed everything. It was now his turn to reciprocate the favor. He helped her out of her nightgown, then carried her over to the bed. She laid down and arched her back up, anticipating what was about to take place.

At first Mike felt guilty about taking advantage of her vulnerability, but seeing her pink gushing pussy staring at him, he couldn't resist. Even if it was just this one time.

"Damn, Mrs. Sasha, you are very wet and smell like strawberries," he said, tasting her juices.

"Call me Sasha," she replied, breathing heavy.

She felt goosebumps forming all over her body as he ate her pussy like it was the last meal on earth. Sasha placed her legs on his shoulders, grabbed his ears, and started rotating her hips in sync with his tongue.

"Mmmmm. Oh, my baby, eat this pussy. It feels soooo good," she moaned, getting close to an orgasm. "I'm about to cum. Faster, baby."

Mike started flicking his tongue over her clit, rapidly bringing her to one of many orgasms to come. After she came, he started sucking on her toes, taking one at a time into his mouth. He licked between each crack, and the bottom, then worked his way up to her stomach. Sasha had a glass of wine sitting on the nightstand. Mike took the rest of it and poured it all over her titties and stomach.

He began licking and sucking every drop of it off of her body. When he reached her navel, he slurped it out like he was drinking from a water fountain. Sasha was so horny by now that she started playing with her pussy and squeezing her nipples.

"No, no, this is my show, baby. You wanted it, so now I'm going to give it to you," Mike replied, moving her hands away.

She smiled and did what he said. He started sucking on her areolas, then stuck two fingers into her pussy.

"When was the last time your husband touched you like this?" he whispered into her ear while rotating his fingers inside of her.

"It's, it's been a long time. Please fuck me now," she pleaded.

Mike turned her over onto her stomach, then spread her legs as far as they could go. When he entered her from behind, Sasha screamed out in pain and pleasure.

"Did you put a condom on?" she asked, lifting her torso in the air for deeper penetration.

"I didn't bring any over here," he answered.

"Just don't cum inside me, okay?"

"I won't," Mike said, grabbing her waist as he started pumping faster and harder like he was trying to bust through her stomach with his dick.

After reaching her second orgasm, Sasha decided to take over. She got up and made Mike lie on his back. Then she got on top of him, straddling him backward so that her back was toward him. She gently placed him inside her and grabbed his ankles. She began riding him like a stallion.

Mike watched her ass bounce up and down on his shaft. Each time it would appear, then disappear like a magic trick. Sasha started making her ass twerk like a stripper. This is what she needed right now, since her husband wouldn't give it to her. She wondered if Mike had ever fucked someone in the ass.

"Have you ever had anal sex?" she asked.

Mike looked at her, shocked because he had never done that before. All the girls he was with were scared to try. Now here was his friend's mom asking him about anal sex.

"No, I've never done that before. It was something that never crossed my mind," he lied.

"Well, it's about time that you learned," she replied, lifting up off of him. She reached inside her dresser and pulled out a tube of lubricant. She placed some all over his dick and put some around the crack of her ass. "Okay, are you ready?"

Mike held his dick in place while she lowered herself onto it. At first it felt tight, but once he was all the way in, it began to loosen up. He started pounding away until he couldn't hold it any longer. As soon as he pulled out, his sperm shot all over her back and ass. Sasha rubbed it over her body, then tasted the salty flavor. Mike was so exhausted that he laid back on the pillow and closed his eyes.

"You have to leave now before my husband or son come home," she said, putting on a robe.

"Okay, but can I come over tomorrow?" he asked, putting his clothes back on.

"I don't know about that, Mike. I'll let you know when the time is right. Let yourself out while I go take a shower," she said, heading for the bathroom.

"Do you want me to join you," he said, following her. She shut the door in his face letting him know her answer.

Mike shook his head and grabbed Sahmeer's clothes. He left that house with more than just a smile on his face. It was something that he would keep to himself. He made up his mind that he was going to see her again, one way or another.

132

$\mathcal{N}$ine

Carla woke up at four o'clock in the morning, once again to an empty bed. Morgan had not been home all night. She sat up in her bed, then turned on the television. To her surprise, a DVD of Morgan and his secretary was still in the player. Carla looked on in shock as her husband had his secretary bent over the desk. She stopped the DVD and tears began to run down her face.

Now it finally registered that her husband was a liar and a cheater. Carla thought to herself that he was probably with Symira right now. She called his cell phone three times but got no answer. She then tried to call Symira and got the same response. Now the only thing that was on her mind was getting revenge, and she knew just who to call. He answered on the second ring.

"Hello," he said, yawning.

"Sorry to wake you up so early, Rapheal. Is this a bad time?" she asked.

"Hey, Carla, it's never a bad time for you to call. What's wrong? I'm up now."

"Are you home? I would like to come over and talk to you about something, but it has to be in person," she said, not wanting to tell him over the phone.

"No, I'm actually in New York, but I will be back tomorrow evening. Is that okay with you?" he said, but he really wasn't in New York.

Disappointed, Carla told him to call when he was back in town. She hung up the phone and sat it down beside her. Interested in seeing everything, Carla started the DVD over and watched it from the beginning.

The more she watched it, the angrier she became. That anger soon turned into her becoming horny. Carla started pinching her nipples. Next she rubbed her pussy lips through the fabric of her pajamas. The moaning sounds from Symira caused her to close her eyes and imagine that it was her making those noises. Within seconds, it became a reality as she started rubbing herself harder and making those same noises.

"Ring, ring, ring." Her phone started going off. She looked at the caller ID and saw that it was Symira.

"Are you with my husband right now?" she said without even saying hello.

"No, I'm actually five minutes away from your house, at my mom's. What's wrong?" Symira said.

"I would like you to come over so we can talk. I just found something, and I want to show it to you."

"I'll be right over," she said, not even hearing the anger in Carla's voice.

"The door will be open. Just come on in," Carla replied before ending the call.

She went downstairs to unlock the door, then returned to her bedroom. She wanted to finish watching the video before Symira arrived. Carla removed her pajamas and got back on the bed. She closed her eyes and started fingering herself, trying to bring herself to orgasm. A couple of minutes later, her juices were pouring all over her fingers. She sighed because she was still horny.

She reached inside her dresser and pulled out her favorite toy. Carla used her vibrating bullet once every two days because that was all the sex she had been getting lately. Being pregnant wasn't helping her hormonic stages either. Just as she turned it on and was about to go to work, Symira walked into her bedroom.

"So is this what you do when the hubby is away?" she asked, standing in the doorway.

Carla put the vibrator down and pulled the sheet over her body.

"I want to know how long you've been fucking my husband," she stated, getting straight to the point.

"I'm not sure what you're talking about. Me and—"

137

"Save the lies, and watch for yourself," Carla said, cutting her off before she finished the lie she was about to tell.

Symira looked at the TV screen and watched as Morgan fucked her on the desk. She didn't know what to say at that moment, so she stayed quiet. Symira thought to herself, why would he leave the DVD out like that?

"That's what I thought. What's the matter, cat got your tongue?" Carla said, looking at the shock on Symira's face. Symira continued to look at the screen.

"Carla, I will do anything for you not to say anything to my husband. He would kill me and Morgan if he found out. I'm begging you not to say anything," she replied, with pleading eyes.

Carla thought about it for a moment, then got up and walked to the foot of the bed. She sat down and removed the sheet that she had covering her. She had on her pajama top and panties.

"Since you want to be fucking my husband behind my back, why don't you fuck me behind his," she said boldly.

Symira looked at her with shock on her face. She thought she was hearing her wrong until she said:

"You wanted to taste it before, so come taste it now, you filthy little whore."

"Well, if you insist," Symira replied, shutting the door.

Symira sat her purse down, then started toward Carla, when she put her hand up, stopping her.

"I want you on your hands and knees, and crawl over here like a dog," Carla said firmly.

Symira got down on her hands and knees, then crawled toward Carla. Carla opened her legs a little as Symira stuck her head between them. She smelled the nice scented aroma

coming from Carla's vagina and got wet instantly.

"Now eat this pussy like your life depended on it. I

want to see what my husband sees in you."

Symira pulled off Carla's panties with her teeth, then

took a quick lick of her clit. Next, she dug in, devouring her

pussy.

Carla's muscles tensed up, then relaxed as her body

started to gyrate to Symira's tongue. She had to admit that

Symira had her tongue game down to a science. She knew

every spot to hit, even hitting some simultaneously. Every

time Symira would hit her G-spot, Carla would cringe from

the sensation. Within the first couple of minutes, Carla had

had at least two orgasms. Symira went deep into her

repertoire. She stuck a finger into Carla's ass and began

flicking her nipples with the other, continuing to suck on her clit.

"Ohhhhhh, yes, that feel so good," Carla said, grabbing the sheet on the bed. It felt like she was being touched by more than one person. When she opened her eyes, someone was standing behind Symira, with her dress hiked up, pumping away. He was playing with one of Carla's breasts while Symira continued to play with the other.

Carla was enjoying it so much, that she didn't even bother to ask who he was and how long he had been standing there. Symira got up and let the man who was behind her move up toward Carla. He aimed his penis, then inserted it into her moist mound. She took all of him without even making a sound. She wrapped her arms around his neck as he sucked on her earlobes.

Symira watched as the man fucked Carla like she was the last piece of pussy on the planet. She sat in one of the chairs, placing one leg on the armrest, then started playing with herself. Each time Carla let out a moan, Symira stuck her finger in deeper, until her whole hand was almost in. Watching them have sex made her cum faster than being involved.

The man turned Carla over on her stomach and entered her from behind. He pumped a few times, getting his dick nice and soaked, then inserted it into her asshole. Carla screamed out as he pushed more and more inside. She put her head into the pillow to muffle the sound. The man spread her ass apart, then fucked her doggy style.

"My God, it hurts. Please slow down some, I'm pregnant," she mumbled.

The man stopped momentarily, getting off the bed. He lifted her off the bed and onto the floor. He got on top of her, then placed his dick back inside of her ass. Carla felt his whole body on top of hers, and her stomach pressed the floor harder than she had anticipated. She tried to pull up some, but he was too big and strong. She cried until he released his sperm inside of her. When he got up, he grabbed his clothes and walked out the door, never even turning around. Symira grabbed the DVD out of the machine and blew Carla a kiss before leaving also.

Carla curled up on the floor in pain, as her stomach started hurting more and more. When she went to get up, there were spots of blood on the floor. She realized what was happening and quickly dialed 911. The ambulance arrived ten minutes later and rushed Carla to the hospital. She left a few hours later after finding out that she had had a miscarriage. Later on that week, she found out that the

guy she had had sex with was actually Symira's husband.

Ten

"**S**o how do you want me to handle this, because it's not going to stop anytime soon," Kyle asked, sitting in the chair, watching the last video that Morgan received.

"I want this harassment to stop before it costs me everything I got. I want you to find this bastard, and put him on ice," he stated, banging his fist on the desk.

"You know what you're asking me to do, right? Once you cross that bridge, there's no turning back," Kyle said.

"If I'm asking too much of you, I can find someone else to handle it. I know exactly what I'm asking you to do. You will be rewarded greatly for this, if you handle it in a timely manner."

Kyle stood up, then extended his hand out to Morgan. They shook hands, and just like that, Morgan had made a deal with the devil.

"Give me forty-eight hours and I'll have the answers you need. Another twenty-four hours and the threat will be eliminated. Just have my money 'cause I would hate to add you to my list," he said before walking out of the office.

When Kyle reached his car, he pulled out the recorder that was hidden in his jacket, and pressed play.

"You know what you're asking me to do, right? Once you cross that bridge, there's no turning back."

"I know exactly what I'm asking. You will be rewarded greatly . . ."

Kyle stopped the tape and smiled to himself. He wanted to keep a record of their conversation just in case Morgan tried to turn on him. If that happened, he wasn't going down alone.

"Just have my money when this is over, or you will be sorry," he said out loud as he pulled out in traffic.

Kyle and Morgan had a mutual friend that introduced them to each other. Kyle had been doing hits since he was sixteen years old, and now at the age of forty-eight, he had over two thousand under his belt. Now it was time to prepare for what may be another one. When he and Morgan talked, they came to an agreement that whoever was behind this extortion was to be eliminated. Now it was his job to do a thorough investigation and eliminate the threat. He figured he would only need three days to complete the task, the most would be a week. He tried never to go past ten days for anything, which most people would say that he rushed it. Until now, though, he had never made a mistake, and hoped that he never did.

* * *

Kevin and Marcus were at Plant Fitness working out, having one of their man-to-man conversations. They did this every Saturday morning, so it was nothing new for the two friends.

"So what's going on with you and the misses?" Kev asked, finishing his rep.

"She's been really quiet lately. I'm scared to go to sleep before her. I think she wants to slit my throat, man, seriously. I would feel better if we were still arguing about everything, but she don't even want to do that."

"You better sleep with one eye open then," Kevin joked.

"That shit ain't funny, man. She crazy as hell. She might be on some Lorena Bobbitt shit, man," Marcus said, putting his hand over his crotch.

Kevin bust out laughing at his friend. Even though they always joked with each other, he knew his friend was really scared.

"You should be okay. I'm sure if she wanted to do something to you, she would have done it already."

"If anything happens to me, make sure she doesn't get to enjoy any of my money," Marcus said nervously.

"Look at that over there," Kevin said, trying to lighten the mood as he pointed to the lady on the treadmill. "You see that camel toe poking out of her tights? That shit is inviting someone to pull it out and taste."

"Fuck the camel toe. Look at her girlfriend's ass. Buffy the Body ain't got shit on that. Neither do Serena, for that matter. I say we go over there and see if they want to have lunch with us," Marcus replied, wiping his face with his towel.

"You don't get enough, do you?"

"It's only lunch. It ain't like I'm trying to fuck her today or something," Marcus stated.

"Well remember what I told you. Now, let's go over there and introduce ourselves," Kevin said, heading toward the ladies.

The two ladies had just finished up on the treadmill when Kevin and Marcus approached them. They looked up and smiled at the two handsome men. Before Marcus could say anything, one of them spoke.

"Hello, Marcus and Kevin. Before y'all get into any trouble, we know your wives," she stated blatantly.

Marcus looked at Kevin with a puzzled face, then turned back to the girls. He was trying to figure out if he had ever seen them before. Kevin was also thinking the same thing but came up empty.

"Have I seen you before?" Marcus asked.

"Not really! We've seen you two, though, at a couple of the games. Our husbands work at the stadium. We sat by your wives a few times while watching the game," the girl stated.

"Oh, so you know that we play ball, huh?" Kevin said.

"Yes, we do. Who doesn't know that? Anyway my name is Allie, and this is Katie. We live in Delaware, near Wilmington," she said.

Allie was a very pretty girl. She stood at five eight, weighed 105 pounds, and she was a white girl. She was wearing black tights and running sneakers. Every man that walked past stared at her pussy because of the way it poked through them.

Katie, on the other hand, was the total opposite. She was thick, with an ass for days. She was five eight, 125 pounds, and she was also a white girl. If you saw her from behind, you would have thought that she was a black girl. All in all, they were two very beautiful women that any man would be proud to call their wife.

"Well, we were just about to head over to the diner across the street and was wondering if you two wanted to join us for lunch. A friendly lunch, that is," Marcus said, noticing the look he was getting.

"You don't have to be so modest. We are big girls. We know how to say yes or no. We're done now and hungry also, so we would love to join y'all for lunch. Your treat, right?" Katie said.

"Of course, I wouldn't have it any other way," Kevin chimed in.

"Well let us take a quick shower and change our clothes. We will meet you there in thirty minutes," Allie told them.

"Sounds good to me. We'll do the same," Kevin said as they all headed toward the shower. "Look at her throwing a little extra in her hips. She's trying to tease us."

"Listen to you, Mr. I Need to Chill Out. You're the one walking with your tongue out like a dog," Marcus joked.

153

"It's just that that white girl got back. I wouldn't mind sampling that right now."

"Play your cards right, and we just might. They're married just like us, so that means no strings attached."

Kevin just shook his head at that thought. She reminded him of Ice T's wife, Coco. He decided that whatever happened after lunch, happened with no regrets. For now, it was time to hit that water so he could be ready.

Thirty minutes later, they were all sitting in the diner waiting for the waitress to bring their food. Allie and Katie both had changed into sundresses. Kevin had on a sweat suit, and Marcus had on a Polo shirt with a pair of True Religion jeans. Once the waitress brought their food, they all ate and chatted for the next forty-five minutes, enjoying each other's conversation.

"Your husband must be one lucky man," Kevin said to Katie. She blushed and told him how true it was.

"So what kind of work do you do?" Marcus asked Allie.

"Well, I work part time at this clothing store, but other than that, I stay home, being a housewife."

"What are you doing after this? I mean, do you have to be home before your husband gets there?" Marcus said.

Allie looked at him like he was speaking in tongues or something. She leaned over and whispered in his ear.

"I have to use the ladies' room. If you're not behind me, you'll blow an opportunity of a lifetime. Excuse me while I powder my nose."

She winked at Katie, who smiled and got up also. They headed toward the bathroom. Marcus and Kevin sat there momentarily. Then, as if on cue, they hopped up and rushed toward the bathroom. When they stepped in, they were greeted with a smile by the girls.

"I see you got the hint," Allie replied, pulling Marcus into a stall. Katie did the same to Kevin.

"This is what I'm talking about," Kevin said, pulling down his sweatpants.

"You're not getting any pussy. I'm just giving you some head, and that's it," she told him, getting on her knees and taking him into her mouth.

He leaned back on the door and grabbed her head as she went to work on his dick. Marcus was in the next stall enjoying the same treatment. When they bust, the girls left them in the bathroom fixing their clothes. They came out, but the girls were gone.

"What the hell just happened?" Kevin asked.

"I believe we just got rewarded for a great lunch," Marcus said with a chuckle.

The two shared a laugh before paying for the food they all ate and heading home. The girls didn't even leave a number so they could call. Marcus hoped he ran into them again so he could finish what they started.

"I can't believe we just did that. You think they will try to find out where we live?" Katie asked while putting more lip gloss on.

"I do hope I run into him again. I wouldn't mind giving him some pussy," Allie stated.

"Me either, just as long as my husband never finds out. I hate sitting in the house all day waiting for him to come home."

"Well, we just have to be discrete about it and not get caught. Now let's get home before we get in trouble."

Katie smiled at what her friend said. She was thinking about how big Kevin was. She had never been with a black guy before, but she definitely was interested in trying it out. Allie was thinking about the same thing. She was squeezing her legs together because her juices were leaking. She planned on practicing with the black dildo she had at home.

* * * *

It had been a little over a month since Carla had lost her baby, and just like she expected, Morgan blamed her for it. She never said anything about seeing the tape or getting even by fucking Symira and the guy that came with her, but she didn't have to, because he already knew.

Symira broke the news to him over pillow talk a few days ago. At first he was pissed, but he decided to use it to his advantage. He was going to cancel the contract that he put out on the person who was extorting him. The problem was, he could not get in touch with him. The phone number that he had was disconnected. He decided to wait for him to make contact with him. He would still give him a quarter of the money, but at least he didn't have to pay it all.

"Are we ever going to talk about what happened to me? You only asked me if I was okay when you brought me home from the hospital," Carla asked Morgan.

"I'm trying to deal with the fact that we're not going to have a son. You know how much I wanted this baby. Why couldn't you stop stressing yourself out? You know that my job requires long hours. How else would we be able to afford this big-ass house or these cars in the driveway, huh?" Morgan said, sitting at the table.

"So you're blaming me for this? I knew you felt that way. Let me tell your lying, cheating, manipulating ass something. I seen the tape of you and that bimbo secretary of yours. What do you have to say about that?"

Morgan laughed because it was time to play his hand. As much as he didn't want to, he said fuck it.

"You shouldn't be insulting Symira like that when you had sex with her the night you lost our baby."

Carla didn't know what to say. She wondered how he even found out about that. "So what, you got hidden cameras in the house now? Let me find out that you're taping everything that goes on in this house."

"I don't have time to talk about this shit right now. If you want to leave, then leave. I'll be back later," Morgan said, heading for the door.

"Where are you going?" she screamed, trying to stop him from leaving.

"Out," was all he said before slamming the door on her.

She leaned on the door and slid to the floor, crying hysterically because she didn't know what to do. She didn't want her family to fall apart, but she was tired of all the shit he was putting her through.

$\mathcal{E}$leven

Nightfall took its sweet time arriving, but when it came, so did the nightly breeze. Akiylah had just walked in the house, when she received a call from Sahmeer. He informed her that he wouldn't be home tonight because he and Mike were going to stay in New York until tomorrow. Exhausted and worn out, she decided to take a quick shower and retire for the night. She didn't even bother to put her panties and bra on afterward as she got under the silk sheets. It didn't take long for her to be counting sheep.

As Akiylah slept peacefully, someone slid in the bed behind her and wrapped his arms around her. Thinking it was Sahmeer, she leaned her body back into his. He became hard when her soft ass swallowed his penis. Trying to tease him a little, she began to move around, bringing him to a full erection. When he felt her pussy, it was soaking wet. He slid inside her from behind, and started slowly pumping in and out.

Akiylah gripped her pillow as she moved her hips to his tempo. It didn't take long for him to explode inside of her. As soon as all the nut was out of him, he slid out of the bed and exited the room. Akiylah found that strange at first, but she thought he went to the bathroom to wash up. She decided to join him, so she grabbed her robe and headed for

the bathroom. Just as she reached the door, Marcus walked

out with a smile on his face.

"Hey, sexy! That thing felt so good tonight. I wish I

didn't bust so soon. I wanted to tear that shit up. Maybe we

can get together this weekend when my wife goes to

Vegas."

Akiylah, now realizing that it wasn't Sahmeer that she

just had sex with, got angry. She squeezed her robe even

tighter, trying not to let him see her body.

"Me don't want to do this anymore," she said.

"As long as you stay under my roof, you will do as I

say, when I say it. If you don't, I will tell my son how

much of a slut you are. Do I make myself clear?" Marcus

asked, walking up on her and untying her robe.

164

She shook her head yes as tears formed in her eyes. Marcus gripped her titties and squeezed them a little harder than normal, before walking back to his room. Akiylah watched the door shut before running into the bathroom to wash the deception off her body.

* * *

Kyle had been watching Morgan and Carla's house for the past week. Morgan had told him that he didn't need the hit carried out anymore because his wife already knew now. He told him that he would give him some money but not the whole thing from the initial agreement. Kyle wasn't trying to hear that, so he decided to get back at Morgan.

Carla came out of the house wearing a skirt and jacket, and hopped into her car. Kyle thought that she was beautiful and wondered why Morgan would cheat on her.

He followed her to a bar that was only right down the street

from where she lived. After parking, she got out and went

inside. Kyle parked across the street from where she

parked, then exited his car, following her inside. She sat at

the far end of the bar, by herself, waiting for her drink.

Kyle sat down next to her and ordered himself a drink also.

"Lovely night, isn't it?" he said to Carla, trying to spark

a conversation.

She looked in his direction but didn't say anything. She

just shook her head and smiled back at him. When their

drinks came, Carla sipped on hers, while Kyle gulped his

down like it was water.

"Let me get another one, and give the lady whatever

she wants," he told the bartender. He put a fifty-dollar bill

on the counter and told her to keep the change.

166

Carla wasn't even halfway through her first glass, but ordered a second one, since he was treating her. She only came out to clear her head, since her husband was going to be out all night on another one of his business trips.

"My name is Brandon. What's yours?" he asked, lying about his name.

"Carla," she replied.

"Well, Carla, what's a married woman doing out here in a bar instead of being home with her husband?"

"Getting a drink, then going back home and waiting for her husband to come home," she said sarcastically.

"Oh, excuse me, feisty lady. I was just asking," Kyle said, throwing his hands in the air.

That caused Carla to smile. For the first time tonight, she thought something or someone was funny. She hadn't been smiling lately, after all. After that, they chatted for a few minutes before Carla excused herself to use the ladies' room.

While she was gone, Kyle reached into his jacket pocket and pulled out a small vial. He placed a couple of drops of the substance inside her drink and then shook it up, hiding the contents. Carla came back and sat down. She finished off her drink, then one more before deciding it was time to leave.

"I have to go home now. Thanks for the drinks and the conversation," she said before getting up and stumbling.

"Whoa, whoa, looks like someone had too much to drink. You can't drive home like that," he said, catching her from falling.

"I'm okay. I only live a couple of blocks from here. I think I'll make it home safely."

"Well, I'm going to make sure. You can leave your car here till tomorrow morning," Kyle stated, helping her to his car.

He looked in her purse to act like he was checking for her address, then hopped in the driver seat.

"Wow, I feel kind of dizzy," Carla said, slurring her words. Her whole surroundings were beginning to spin, leaving her confused and tired.

Kyle sat there, momentarily watching Carla transform before his eyes. His dick started to get harder and harder as he thought of what was getting ready to take place soon. He pulled away from the bar, driving slowly down the street. He kept glancing at Carla to see if the drug had fully taken its effect yet.

Carla was in somewhat of a trance, and her eyes rolled toward the back of her head. He knew then that she was completely out of it. Taking full advantage of the skirt she was wearing, Kyle roughly shoved his hand between her legs, moving her panties to the side. Carla was totally passed out by now and couldn't feel his fingers going in and out of her pussy. He slowly licked his fingers, tasting her juices as he pulled them out of her.

"Damn, I can't wait to get this bitch to her house," he said to himself.

After the short drive, they had reached their destination, and Carla was unaware of what the night had in store. He helped her out of the car and into the house. He laid her on the couch and had his way with her for the next thirty minutes.

When Carla woke up, all of her clothes had been torn off, and her ass was burning with pain. She had been violated in every hole on her body. She was embarrassed

170

and ashamed because she couldn't remember anything except being at the bar with a strange guy. That's when it hit her, and she realized what had happened. She had been sexually assaulted by the man she thought was nice.

She ran upstairs and took a shower, trying to wash his smell off of her. She called her husband to inform him of what had happened, and he told her to go straight to the hospital and he'd meet her there. Little did she know that she had already washed all the DNA off, so it would be hard to find out who did it. All she had to go on was a first name, which was a fake name.

While she was at the hospital, she had all types of tests run on her. She refused the rape kit because she didn't know what to do, and her husband never even showed up, which pissed her off even more. All the tests came back negative, and it felt like a big burden was lifted for Carla.

She went home, but the worst was still to come.

welve

It had been a few months since Sasha had slept with her son's best friend. Mike would come over, but she would act like nothing ever happened. Deep down inside, though, she actually wanted to do it again. For some strange reason, she couldn't stop thinking about him, or his penis, for that matter.

She had just returned from getting her hair done, when she noticed that the house was once again empty.

"Marcus, Sahmeer, are you home?" she yelled out, with no answer. She grabbed the mail and sat at the kitchen table to go through it.

While looking through the bills, she stumbled across a card. She opened it up and all it said was:

Sasha,

Meet me at the Inn of the Dove tonight at 8 PM. I have a surprise for you.

Love,

You know who

She smiled because she thought Marcus was trying to make up for everything once again. Sasha looked at the clock and realized that she only had an hour and a half to get ready. She rushed upstairs and pulled out her Victoria Secret thong set and one of her pencil dresses that accentuated her every curve. She took a shower, got dressed, and was out the door in no time.

When she arrived at the hotel, she didn't see her husband's car. The person at the front desk gave her a key card and told her that the person she was meeting was waiting in the room for her. She approached the door, ready to give Marcus the time of his life.

"Hello, Mrs. Sasha," someone said, causing her to turn around, startled.

When she saw who it was, she almost lost her breath. She backed up against the door, surprised for sure.

"Mike, what are you doing here?" she asked, confused.

"I'm the one that summoned you to meet me here. I haven't been able to stop thinking about you since that night in your room. Even though we both know this is wrong, it feels so right, and I want one more night with you," Mike said, moving closer to her.

Before she could respond, he backed her up against the door of the room and pressed a kiss to her lips. As much as she wanted to resist, the heat coming from between her legs said differently. Sasha wrapped both of her arms around his neck, kissing on his earlobes and face. She moaned against his mouth. He was strong, and his powerful arms squeezed her tight against his upper torso, but it wasn't discomfort that drove out the moan. It was the longing she felt for him.

He drew her into his arms and turned so that he was now leaning on the door. He passionately kissed her like it was his last kiss on earth, lifting her off the ground and holding her ass in the palm of his hands.

She wrapped her legs around his waist as he slid her thong to the side, entering her while they were still outside the room. Sasha started sucking on his bottom lip as she moved up and down on his shaft. The heat coming from their bodies made Sasha want to rip his and her clothes off right there for all to see.

Mike managed to slide the key card into the door, opening it up so they could go inside. He carried her over to the hotel bed. They both fell down, letting the momentum land them softly on the mattress. Both of them laughed while still kissing one another.

Sasha began to undress him because her pussy needed a beating, and the longer she waited, the more desperate she became. The desire for him took over her more reserved distinguishing quality. She ripped his shirt open and helped him out of his skinny jeans. Her left hand caressed his shoulder and upper back muscles while her right hand roamed over his chest and lower abdominal muscles. She then helped him out of his boxers and lay on the bed.

He grabbed her legs and pulled her toward him. He pulled her dress up to her waist, not wanting to wait any longer. He pulled off her thong, exposing her cleanly shaven vagina. When he entered her wet hole this time, it sucked all the air out of her. She exploded in ecstacy, and it was only the first of many more to come.

Next he scooted down between her legs because he wanted to taste the nectar coming from her sweet pot. He started off with a slow-motion technique, then sped up, sending her into all types of convulsions. Sasha was enjoying everything this young man had to offer. She felt like a cougar, even though she was only in her thirties. He was giving her everything that her husband didn't have the time to do. Even though there was a big chance of them getting caught, she didn't care right now.

Mike was sucking and licking on her labia like it was an oyster. After she reached another orgasm, she decided it was time to reciprocate the favor. She grabbed his dick and spit all over it, before placing the head into her mouth. The tongue ring that she had increased the sensation times ten. She continued to suck him until he exploded all down her throat.

"That was the most incredible blowjob I ever had," Mike informed her.

"Well, you need to come back to life, 'cause I need another dose before I go home," she replied, stroking his limp dick.

"Keep that up, and it will be on in a couple of minutes," Mike said, feeling himself growing again.

Sasha's sex drive was at an all-time high right now. She knew her period was about to come on, so she was going to get as much as she could tonight. They had wild sex until around 3:00 a.m. before heading back home. When she got home, the house was still empty. She went straight to bed with a beautiful smile on her face.

* * *

Morgan was so drunk last night that the intoxicating smell came out of his pores like a faucet. He didn't know what to do ever since his wife was raped. No one knew who did it but her, and the name that she said could have been anybody's. She was still mad at him for not showing up at the hospital. He was sleeping in the guest room. Symira hadn't had sex with him ever since that night they talked about her sleeping with Carla. It seemed as if everything was falling apart in his life.

The governor gave him an ultimatum that either he get his act together or lose his job. The governor didn't need all the negative publicity that Morgan would end up bringing if the media got wind of the stuff he was doing. Since it was his first term, the governor put Morgan on a ninety-day probation. If there wasn't a significant amount of improvement, he was gone. So he had his work cut out for him, and the cheating was going to be his greatest challenge.

When he got home, Carla was sitting on the couch, watching the television. She didn't even bother to look up in his direction as he entered the living room area.

"How are you doing?" he asked.

"Fine."

"That's all you're going to say to me? It's been weeks, and you still won't talk to me. Baby, I'm sorry for not being there when you needed me the most. I was stuck in traffic, but I did get here to be with you. Can you please forgive me?"

She looked up and saw the sincerity in his eyes. That was a look she hadn't seen in years. It melted her heart because she wanted to make things right with her husband.

"I just don't know what you want me to do. We both made some mistakes, but yours was greater than mine, and I still forgave you. You weren't there when I needed you the most. That hurts more than anything."

Morgan kneeled down by her side. "Please forgive me for that. I will never let anything come between us again, I promise."

"That remains to be seen. If you really mean what you say, you have a lot of making up to do. Just know that I'm not just going to jump back into your arms, so don't look for any affection from me anytime soon," she said with a smirk. That led Morgan to believe that he would be making love to his wife again real soon.

"So what are you doing tomorrow? Do you have any plans, because I would like to take you with me to Harrisburg. I have to prepare a speech for the governor," Mike said.

"Yes, I'm actually busy. I have some things to do with Michelle. We are going to Delaware to look at some properties."

"Why? Sasha not going with her?"

"What's with all the questions? She will be at the office helping her mom out. We're just starting over. Don't ruin it before it even has a chance to get anywhere."

"I'm just asking because I know how close they are, but I'm going to mind my business. I'll be in the den working on some of the speech if you need me," Morgan stated, leaving before they started arguing.

After he left, Carla picked up her cell phone and dialed a number. The caller answered after the fourth ring.

"Hello."

"Are we still meeting today? I don't have anything going on at the moment," she said.

"Sure, we can meet at our regular spot. I might be running a little behind because I have a few things to pick up, but I will be there, so don't you go anywhere, okay?"

"Okay, I'll be waiting. See you in a few then," Carla answered before ending the call.

She grabbed her purse and car keys, then headed out the door. Morgan looked out the window just in time to see her pulling out of the driveway. He decided that since the speech wasn't due until tomorrow, he would just go to the gym for a couple of hours. He felt like there was no need to sit in the house doing nothing by himself. He quickly changed his clothes and grabbed his keys before heading out.

* * *

Carla pulled up to the building at around 7:30 p.m. When she tried to open the door, it was locked, so she tried the side door, which was unlocked. When she made it to the back of the center, Rapheal was waiting to greet her with a candlelight dinner.

"Welcome to your graduation ceremony," he stated briefly, giving her a little kiss on the cheek.

"You did this for me? You are so sweet. I don't deserve any of this," she said, sitting down.

"You deserve everything plus some more after all that you've been through. I'm sorry that that no good man treated you the way he has. I want to tell you something," he said, pouring both of them a drink before continuing.

"When I was fourteen years old, I accidentally substituted salt for sugar in a cake recipe. I baked the cake, put a lemon icing on it, and served it to my mom and other family members. It looked like a cake, but as soon as you tasted it, you knew something else was going on. Carla, people are like that too. Sometimes you just can't tell

186

what's on the inside from looking at the outside. Sometimes people are just one big surprise just like that salt cake that I made. Sometimes it turns out to be good, sometimes bad, and sometimes the surprise is just fucking confusing. The thing is, you have to experience the bad in order to get the good."

Carla listened intently to what Rapheal was saying. She didn't know that he was so deep. She decided to try and make some sense out of it all.

"Why did you tell me all of that?"

"Because there is a good man out there for you, but you keep deciding to stay with that scum. Open your eyes, Carla, because that person won't wait around for too long. Now let's enjoy this fine dinner that I made for us," he stated.

For the rest of their time together, Carla thought about everything he had said to her. She even wondered if that someone that he spoke of was him. She hoped that he didn't just look at her as collateral damage, because she wasn't looking for a sympathy relationship. She wanted more, and Morgan fucked up this time. It was over for good, and no one would change her mind this time. They ate and played music for hours before Carla went home and went straight to bed.

Thirteen

When Sasha woke up the next morning, Marcus had already left for practice. Sahmeer and Akiylah were still in bed asleep. She went downstairs and into the kitchen to make some coffee. There was a loaf of raisin bread on the counter, so she made some toast, then put butter and jelly on it. She enjoyed her toast and coffee before going back upstairs to get dressed.

Sasha showered and got dressed before swiping some mascara on her lashes, and took off out the door. The papers that her mom gave her the day before were sitting on the passenger seat when she got in. She was going to help her mom out at the office today just to kill some time.

When she arrived at the office, her mom was talking to someone on the phone. She sat down in one of the chairs and waited until she was finished with her conversation.

"You are very perplexed right now, and I need you to be on the same page as the rest of us. They breached the contract, and that information will be permissible in court. Call me with all the details when you get them. I'm on my way to the courthouse right now," she said, hanging up the phone.

"Hey, Mom, how are you?" Sasha asked.

"I'm fine! Glad to see you made it. Just sit in my office and take all the calls for me while I'm gone. My new secretary will be in at noon. Then you can run everything until I get back."

"Why can't they answer the calls?" Sasha complained.

"Because they have other things to do that require all their time and energy. I know you wouldn't want to do it anyway. Just sit in here and relax till the secretary comes. Be the boss that I've trained you to be. Love you," she said, giving Sasha a kiss and rushing out the door.

For the next few minutes, Sasha sat in her mother's office answering calls. She was getting bored by the minute. She was playing blackjack online, when the phone rang.

"Good afternoon, thank you for calling Miller's Real Estate. This is Sasha. How may I help you?"

"What are you wearing right now, sexy?" the caller asked.

"Who is this asking me that?" she said, confused.

"This is your secret lover. Now, I'm gonna ask you one more time before I hang up. What are you wearing with your sexy self?"

Sasha finally recognized the voice and smiled. She decided to play the game with him.

"I'm wearing a miniskirt and a blouse. Why are you asking me that, and how did you know I was here?" she said seductively.

"Your son told me that no one would be home today and asked did I want to come play Call of Duty with him. I asked where you were going to be, and he said there."

"So what do I owe the privilege of this call?" she asked, tapping the pen on the desk.

"I just wanted to see if you were scared to have phone sex or not."

"Listen, you're like my second son. We is not supposed to be doing this, so we need to end this."

"You know the sound of my voice is making you wet as we speak. Plus, I think it's too late to be looking at me as your son, don't you? Why don't you just lift that skirt up and stick a finger in that good pussy, then taste it, and tell me what it taste like," Mike said. He started smiling because he knew he had her when she didn't say anything or hang up.

Sasha leaned back in the chair, looked around making sure nobody was paying her any attention, and then lifted her skirt up half way. She stuck her hand inside her panties and started fingering herself.

"Hello, are you there?" Mike asked.

193

He got his answer when he heard her breathing heavy on the phone. She took one leg and put it on the desk, exposing her vagina more and giving her more access to her tunnel.

"That's right, baby. I hear you. Place the phone down there so I can hear that squishy noise."

Just as she was about to do it, she felt herself getting sick. She was about to throw up. She hung the phone up, then hurried to the bathroom. Soon as she made it to a stall, it all came out of her body and into the toilet. She was wondering what had caused it because she hadn't even eaten anything except the toast this morning. After rinsing her mouth out, she looked in the mirror, and that's when it hit her.

"Oh my God, I better not be," she said to herself.

* * *

Kevin and Katie had been seeing a lot of each other lately. They would sneak around whenever they had a chance to get away from their spouses. Just like with any other women, he was getting tired of her.

BOOKS BY GOOD2GO AUTHORS

GOOD 2 GO FILMS PRESENTS

**THE HAND I WAS DEALT- FREE WEB SERIES
NOW AVAILABLE ON YOUTUBE!
YOUTUBE.COM/SILKWHITE212**

SEASON TWO NOW AVAILABLE

To order books, please fill out the order form below:

To order films please go to ***www.good2gofilms.com***

Name:_____

Address:_____

City: _____ State: _____ Zip Code: _____

Phone:_____

Email:_____

Method of Payment: Check   VISA   MASTERCARD

Credit Card#:_____

Name as it appears on card: _____

Signature: _____

Item Name	Price	Qty	Amount
48 Hours to Die – Silk White	$14.99		
A Hustler's Dream - Ernest Morris	$14.99		
A Hustler's Dream 2 - Ernest Morris	$14.99		
Business Is Business – Silk White	$14.99		
Business Is Business 2 – Silk White	$14.99		
Business Is Business 3 – Silk White	$14.99		
Childhood Sweethearts – Jacob Spears	$14.99		
Childhood Sweethearts 2 – Jacob Spears	$14.99		
Childhood Sweethearts 3 - Jacob Spears	$14.99		
Childhood Sweethearts 4 - Jacob Spears	$14.99		
Flipping Numbers – Ernest Morris	$14.99		
Flipping Numbers 2 – Ernest Morris	$14.99		
He Loves Me, He Loves You Not - Mychea	$14.99		
He Loves Me, He Loves You Not 2 - Mychea	$14.99		
He Loves Me, He Loves You Not 3 - Mychea	$14.99		
He Loves Me, He Loves You Not 4 – Mychea	$14.99		
He Loves Me, He Loves You Not 5 – Mychea	$14.99		
Lord of My Land – Jay Morrison	$14.99		
Lost and Turned Out – Ernest Morris	$14.99		
Married To Da Streets – Silk White	$14.99		
M.E.R.C. - Make Every Rep Count Health and Fitness	$14.99		
My Besties – Asia Hill	$14.99		
My Besties 2 – Asia Hill	$14.99		
My Besties 3 – Asia Hill	$14.99		
My Besties 4 – Asia Hill	$14.99		
My Boyfriend's Wife - Mychea	$14.99		
My Boyfriend's Wife 2 – Mychea	$14.99		
Naughty Housewives – Ernest Morris	$14.99		
Naughty Housewives 2 – Ernest Morris	$14.99		
Naughty Housewives 3 – Ernest Morris	$14.99		
Never Be The Same – Silk White	$14.99		

Stranded – Silk White	$14.99		
Slumped – Jason Brent	$14.99		
Tears of a Hustler - Silk White	$14.99		
Tears of a Hustler 2 - Silk White	$14.99		
Tears of a Hustler 3 - Silk White	$14.99		
Tears of a Hustler 4- Silk White	$14.99		
Tears of a Hustler 5 – Silk White	$14.99		
Tears of a Hustler 6 – Silk White	$14.99		
The Panty Ripper - Reality Way	$14.99		
The Panty Ripper 3 – Reality Way	$14.99		
The Solution – Jay Morrison	$14.99		
The Teflon Queen – Silk White	$14.99		
The Teflon Queen 2 – Silk White	$14.99		
The Teflon Queen 3 – Silk White	$14.99		
The Teflon Queen 4 – Silk White	$14.99		
The Teflon Queen 5 – Silk White	$14.99		
The Teflon Queen 6 - Silk White	$14.99		
The Vacation – Silk White	$14.99		
Tied To A Boss - J.L. Rose	$14.99		
Tied To A Boss 2 - J.L. Rose	$14.99		
Tied To A Boss 3 - J.L. Rose	$14.99		
Time Is Money - Silk White	$14.99		
Two Mask One Heart – Jacob Spears and Trayvon Jackson	$14.99		
Two Mask One Heart 2 – Jacob Spears and Trayvon Jackson	$14.99		
Two Mask One Heart 3 – Jacob Spears and Trayvon Jackson	$14.99		
Young Goonz – Reality Way	$14.99		
Young Legend – J.L. Rose	$14.99		
Subtotal:			
Tax:			
Shipping (Free) U.S. Media Mail:			
Total:			

Make Checks Payable To:
Good2Go Publishing
7311 W Glass Lane,
Laveen, AZ 85339

CPSIA information can be obtained
at www.ICGtesting.com
Printed in the USA
LVOW03s2248070917
547918LV00001B/12/P